Les Belles Images

Simone de Beauvoir, Europe's leading woman novelist, was born in Paris in 1909. A life-long friend of writer and philosopher Jean-Paul Sartre, her books are famous throughout the world.

The Second Sex, published in 1952, was hailed as a revolutionary study of the sexual nature of women. *The Mandarins*, her remarkably frank portrait of the post-war intellectual élite in France, won the coveted Prix Goncourt and was described by Iris Murdoch as 'a novel on the grand scale . . . a superb document containing analyses of great brilliance.'

Les Belles Images is a profound and highly perceptive novel which lays bare the corruption beneath the glossy surface of modern society.

'Consistently readable : . . The theme is the impact of the *real* world on a successful little group of rich bourgeois who are determined to keep it out.'

Cyril Connolly, Sunday Times

'The lucid, exact, but warm and easy writing of Simone de Beauvoir, the subtlety of her psychological understanding of old and young, always give me ir

Post

**Available in Fontana
by the same author**

She Came to Stay
The Woman Destroyed
The Mandarins

Les Belles Images

Simone de Beauvoir

Translated by Patrick O'Brian

Fontana/Collins

First published in France by Editions Gallimard
under the title *Les Belles Images* 1966
First published in Great Britain by Wm. Collins
Sons and Co. Ltd. 1968
First issued in Fontana Books 1969
Sixth Impression October 1977

© in the French edition, Editions Gallimard
1966
© in the English translation, Wm. Collins
Sons & Co. Ltd., London & Glasgow and
G. P. Putnam's Sons, New York, 1968

Made and printed in Great Britain by
Richard Clay (The Chaucer Press) Ltd.,
Bungay, Suffolk

To Claude Lanzman

CHAPTER 1

'This really is an astonishing October,' said Gisèle Dufrène: they nodded agreement; they smiled, a summer
heat flooded down from the blue-grey sky (What have the
others got that I haven't?), their eyes glided over the un-
flawed picture that the glossy magazines *Plaisir de
France* and *Votre Maison* had reproduced—the farm-
house bought for a song, or at least shall we say for an
aria, and done up by Jean-Charles at the cost of a grand
opera ('Don't worry about the odd million,' Gilbert had
said), the roses against the stone wall, the chrysanthe-
mums, the asters, the dahlias, 'the loveliest in the whole
of the Ile-de-France,' said Dominique; the screen and the
blue and violet armchairs (so daring!) made their contrast with the green of the lawn, the ice tinkled in the
glasses, Houdan kissed Dominique's hand as she sat there,
very slim in her black trousers and her brilliant shirt, her
pale hair something between blonde and white—from
behind you would say she was no more than thirty.
'Dominique, no one is such a good hostess as you.' (At this
very moment in another garden, wholly different and
exactly the same someone else is saying these words and
the same smile is forming on another face: 'What a wonderful Sunday!' Why do I think that?)

Everything had been perfect, the sun and the wafting
air, the barbecue, the thick steaks, the salad, the wine.
Gilbert had told stories about travel and hunting in
Kenya and then he had become absorbed in this Japanese
puzzle—he still had six pieces to fit in—and Laurence
had suggested an intelligence test, the one about the man
who takes you over the frontier: it was a great success, for
they had absolutely loved being astonished at themselves
and laughing at one another. She had given out a great

7

deal and that was why she was feeling depressed now: I'm a manic-depressive. Louise was playing with her cousins at the far end of the garden; Catherine was reading in front of the leaping little fire: she looked just like all other small girls who lie on hearthrugs, happily reading. Don Quixote: last week it was Quentin Durward. It was never *that* which made her weep at night: what was it, then? Louise was all upset: 'Mama, Catherine is sad about something; she cries in the night.' She liked the teachers at school; she had a new friend; she was well; the house was cheerful.

'Still looking for a slogan?' said Dufrène.

'I have to persuade people to panel their walls with wood.'

It was convenient: whenever her mind wandered they thought she was trying to hit on a slogan. The talk around her was about Jeanne Texcier's attempted suicide. With a cigarette in her left hand and with her open right hand in the air as though to stop anyone interrupting, Dominique said in her commanding, well-modulated voice, 'She's not particularly bright—it was her husband who made her career; but even so, when you're one of the most talked-about women in Paris you don't go and behave like a shop-girl!'

In another garden, wholly different and exactly the same, someone said, 'Dominique Langlois? It was Gilbert Mortier who made her career.' And that was unfair: she had got into radio by the side door in '45 and she had succeeded by the sweat of her brow, working like a black and trampling over anyone who stood in her way. Why do they take such a delight in pulling one another to pieces? They say—and Gisèle Dufrène certainly thinks it—that Mama hooked Gilbert with an eye to the main chance: all right, so she could never have afforded this house and her travelling without him; but what he gave her was something quite different. After all she was terribly at a loss after leaving Papa (he wandered about the house like a soul in torment: how callously she walked

8

out the minute Marthe was married), and it was thanks to Gilbert that she became this completely self-assured woman. (Of course, you could say ...)

Hubert and Marthe came back from the woods, carrying huge bunches of leaves. With her head thrown back and a fixed smile on her lips she walked with a light and happy step—a saint drunk with the joyful love of God, that was the role she had been playing ever since she had found the faith. They sat down again on the blue and violet cushions. Hubert lit his pipe: he was certainly the only man left in France who called it 'my old puffer'. His GPI grin: his fatness. He wore black sunglasses when he was travelling. 'I love to travel incognito.' A very good dentist, who earnestly studied the daily double in his spare time. I can quite see that Marthe should want to discover something in the way of compensation.

'In Europe in the summer you won't find a single beach with enough room to lie down,' said Dominique. 'In Bermuda there are huge stretches, almost empty; and nobody knows you.'

'Your really choice little place, ha ha,' said Laurence.

'And what about Tahiti? Why didn't you go back to Tahiti?' asked Gisèle.

'In 1955 Tahiti was fine. Now it's worse than Saint-Tropez. Commonplace, but commonplace...'

Twenty years back. Papa would suggest Florence or Granada: she would say 'Everybody goes there; it's commonplace, but commonplace...' The four of them trundling about in the car—it was like a family in a comic strip, she said. He travelled in Greece and Italy without us, and we spent our holidays in fashionable places—at least what Dominique used to think fashionable in those days. Now she crosses the Atlantic to sun-bathe. Gilbert is going to take her to Baalbek for Christmas...

'They say there are splendid beaches in Brazil with nobody on them,' said Gisèle. 'And you can run over to Brasilia. How I should love to see Brasilia!'

'Oh no!' said Laurence. 'Those enormous complexes

9

outside Paris are depressing enough already. Imagine a whole city built on the same lines!'

'You're a good-old-days creature, like your father,' said Dominique.

'Who isn't?' said Jean-Charles. 'Even in these days of rockets and automation people still retain the same state of mind they had in the nineteenth century.'

'Not me,' said Dominique.

'As for you,' said Gilbert in a tone of conviction (or rather of grandiloquence, for he always kept a certain distance from his words), 'you are always exceptional.'

'At all events the workmen who built the town are of my opinion: they didn't choose to leave their wooden houses.'

'They scarcely had the choice, Laurence dear,' said Gilbert. 'The rents in Brazilia are far beyond their reach.' His mouth rounded in a slight smile, as though he were apologizing for his greater powers.

'Brasilia is quite out of date today,' said Dufrène. 'It's still an architecture in which roofs, doors, walls, chimneys and so on have a separate existence. What we are trying to create now is the synthesized house in which each element is polyvalent—the roof merges into the wall and flows down into the middle of the patio.'

Laurence was cross with herself: what she had said was silly, of course. That's where talking about things you don't really understand gets you. 'Never talk about what you are not familiar with,' said Mlle Houchet. But in that case you would never open your mouth. She listened in silence as Jean-Charles described the city of the future. Incomprehensibly it enchanted him, all these wonders to come that he would never see with his own eyes. It had delighted him to learn that the man of today was some inches taller than the man of the middle ages, who in his turn was taller than prehistoric man. How lucky they are to be able to feel all this enthusiasm. Once again, and still with the same ardour, Dufrène and Jean-Charles were arguing about the crisis in architecture.

10

'Funds have to be provided, of course,' said Jean-Charles, 'but by other means. Giving up the force of dissuasion would mean falling outside the context of history.'

Nobody replied: in the silence there arose Marthe's inspired voice, 'If only the nations would all agree to disarm together! Have you read Paul VI's latest message?'

Dominique interrupted her impatiently. 'Absolutely qualified people have assured me that if war breaks out it will only need twenty years for mankind to be back at the present level.'

Gilbert looked up: he only had four pieces left unplaced. 'There won't be a war. The gap between the capitalist and socialist countries will soon be done away with. Because now we're in the great twentieth-century revolution: producing is more important than possessing.'

Then why spend so much on armaments, thought Laurence. But Gilbert would know the answer to that one and she had no desire to be made a fool of again. Besides, Jean-Charles had already replied: without the bomb we should fall outside the context of history. What exactly did that mean? It would certainly be something very dreadful, for everybody looked most concerned.

Gilbert turned towards her with a pleasant smile. 'You must come on Friday. I want you to hear my new hi-fi.'

'The same as Karim's and Alexander of Yugoslavia's,' said Dominique.

'It really is astonishing,' said Gilbert. 'Once you've heard it, you can't listen to music on an ordinary system any more.'

'Then I don't want to hear it,' said Laurence. 'I love listening to music.' (That is not really true. I'm saying it to be funny.)

Jean-Charles seemed deeply interested. 'How much must you reckon, at the lowest figure, for a good hi-fi installation?'

'At the minimum, the strict minimum, you can get a mono set-up for three hundred thousand old francs. But it's not the real thing, not the real thing at all.'

'To have something really good, I suppose you have to pay round about a million?' said Dufrène.

'Listen: a good system in mono costs between six hundred thousand and a million. In stereo, say two million. I advise mono rather than not very good stereo. A worth-while combination-amplifier costs something in the neighbourhood of five hundred thousand.'

'That's what I said, a minimum of a million,' said Dufrène, sighing.

'There are sillier ways of spending a million,' said Gilbert.

'If Vergne gets the Roussillon job, I'll get us one,' said Jean-Charles to Laurence. He turned to Dominique. 'He has quite a terrific idea for one of those vacation-complexes they're building down there.'

'Vergne does have terrific ideas. But they aren't often carried out,' said Dufrène.

'They will be. Do you know him?' Jean-Charles asked Gilbert. 'It's fascinating to work with him—the whole studio is alive with enthusiasm. You don't just plod along, you create.'

'He is the greatest architect of his generation,' laid down Dominique. 'The front rank of the avant-garde in town-planning.'

'I'd still rather be with Monnod,' said Dufrène. 'You don't create; you plod along. Only you make much more money.'

Hubert took his pipe out of his mouth. 'That's a point.'

Laurence stood up: she smiled at her mother. 'Can I rob you of some of your dahlias?'

'Of course.'

Marthe had got up too; she walked off with her sister. 'You saw Papa on Wednesday? How is he?'

'At home he's always cheerful. He argued with Jean-Charles, by way of a change.'

'Jean-Charles doesn't understand Papa either.' Marthe gazed heavenwards. 'He's so different from other people. In his own way Papa does reach the supernatural. Music, poetry ... for him, it's a prayer.'

Laurence bent over the dahlias: this kind of talk embarrassed her. Certainly, he has something that other people don't possess, that I don't possess (but what in fact have they got that I haven't?). She tightened her grip upon the splendid dahlias: pink, red, yellow, tawny.

'A happy day, my pets?' asked Dominique.

'Wonderful,' cried Marthe earnestly.

'Wonderful,' repeated Laurence.

The light was fading; she would not be sorry to go in. She hesitated. She had waited until the last moment: asking her mother for something made her feel as nervous now as it had done when she was fifteen. 'I've something to ask you ...'

'What is it?' Dominique's voice was cold.

'It's about Serge. He wants to leave the university. He'd like to get a job on the radio or television.'

'Was it your father who gave you that message?'

'I met Bernard and Georgette at Papa's.'

'How are they getting along? Still playing Darby and Joan?'

'Oh, I only saw them for a moment.'

'Tell your father once and for all that I'm not an employment agency. I think it's an absolute shame the way people try to exploit me. For my part I've never asked anyone for anything.'

'You can scarcely blame Papa for wanting to help his nephew,' said Marthe.

'I blame him for not being able to do anything himself.' Dominique waved aside all objections. 'If he were a mystic, if he'd become a Trappist, I should understand. [No you wouldn't, thought Laurence.] But he's chosen mediocrity.'

She could not forgive him for having become a parliamentary draftsman instead of the famous barrister she had thought she was marrying. A complete side-issue, she said.

'It's late,' said Laurence. 'I must go up and titivate.'

'I'll come too; I'm going to change,' said Dominique.

'I'll see to the children,' said Marthe.

It was convenient: ever since she had entered saint-hood she had monopolized all the unpleasant chores. She derived such lofty joys from it that there was no need to feel guilty about leaving them to her.

As she brushed her hair in her mother's room—such pretty stuff, this Spanish provincial—Laurence made a last effort for Serge.

'You really can't do anything for Serge?'

'No.'

Dominique came nearer the looking-glass. 'I look aw-ful. At my age a woman who works all day and goes out every evening is utterly done for. I ought to sleep.'

Laurence examined her mother in the mirror. The per-fect, the ideal picture of a woman who is ageing well. Who is ageing. It was a picture Dominique would not accept. For the first time she was showing weakness—flinching. Hitherto she had taken the lot, illnesses, hard knocks, everything. And now suddenly there was panic in her eyes.

'I can't believe that one day I'll be seventy.'

'There's no woman who stands up to it as well as you do,' said Laurence.

'My body's all right; I don't envy anyone. But look here.' She pointed to her eyes, and her neck. Obviously, she was no longer in her forties.

'You aren't in your twenties any more, obviously,' said Laurence. 'But lots of men prefer women who know their way about. Take Gilbert...'

'Gilbert... It's to keep him that I destroy myself going out all the time. The danger is that it may turn against me.'

'Oh, come now!'

Dominique put on her Balenciaga suit. Never anything from Chanel: you spend a fortune to look as if you dressed at a second-hand stall. 'That cow Marie-Claire,' she murmured. 'She obstinately refuses to divorce: just for the pleasure of bitching me.'

'Perhaps she'll give way in the end.'

There was no sort of doubt that Marie-Claire said 'that cow Dominique'. In the days of Lucile de Saint-Chamont Gilbert still lived with his wife: the question did not even arise, since Lucile had children and a husband. Dominique had made him leave Marie-Claire: if he had yielded it was because it suited him, fair enough; but even so Laurence had thought her mother pretty savage.

'Of course, there are a good many risks attached to living with Gilbert. He likes his freedom.'

'And so do you.'

'Yes.'

Dominique twirled in front of the triple mirror and smiled. In fact she was delighted to be going to dine at the Verdelets': a minister—that really does impress her. How ill-natured I am, said Laurence to herself. Dominique was her mother: she was fond of her. But she was also a stranger. Who was hiding behind those reflections that spun in the mirrors? Maybe nobody at all.

'How are things with you? All right?'

'Splendid. I go from one triumph to another.'

'And the children?'

'As you saw, thriving.'

Dominique asked questions as a matter of principle; but she would have thought it quite improper if Laurence gave disturbing or even detailed answers.

In the garden Jean-Charles was leaning over Gisèle's chair: a trivial flirtation that pleased both of them (and Dufrène too, I believe); they gave one another the impression that they might have the affair that neither of them wanted. (And what if they were to have it, by any chance? I believe I shouldn't mind it at all. So there can be love without jealousy?)

'I count on you for Friday, then,' said Gilbert. 'It's no

fun when you aren't there.'

'Oh, come!'

'It's quite true.'

He shook Laurence's hand very warmly, as though there were a particular understanding between them: that was why everyone thought he had charm.

'Until Friday.'

People loved having Laurence: they loved going to her place: she really could not understand why.

'A wonderful day,' said Gisèle.

'With the life one leads in Paris, one absolutely has to have this relaxation,' said Jean-Charles.

'It's essential,' said Gilbert.

Laurence settled the children into the back of the car, locked their doors and got in beside Jean-Charles: they drove down the lane behind Dufrène's Citroën DS.

'The astonishing thing about Gilbert is that he remains so unpretentious,' said Jean-Charles: 'When you think of his responsibilities—his power. And not the slightest trace of pomp.'

'He can do without it.'

'You don't like him: that's perfectly natural. But don't be unfair.'

'Oh, but I do like him. [Did she like him or not? She liked everybody.] Gilbert doesn't hold forth, it's true,' she said. 'But everybody knows that he runs one of the two biggest electronics companies in the world, and everyone knows the part he played in setting up the Common Market.'

'I wonder what his income is,' said Jean-Charles. 'Virtually unlimited.'

'It would frighten me to have so much money.'

'He uses it intelligently.'

'Yes.'

It was odd: when Gilbert talked about his travels he was very amusing indeed. An hour later you couldn't put your finger on what he had said.

'A thoroughly successful week-end!' said Jean-Charles.

16

'Thoroughly successful.'

And once again Laurence wondered what have the others got that I haven't? Oh, there was no point in worrying about it; there were days like that, when everything was wrong from the word go and you took no pleasure in anything whatever: she ought to be used to it. Yet every time she examined herself—what's wrong? Sudden indifference, remoteness, as though she did not belong among them at all. Her nervous breakdown of five years back had been explained to her; quantities of young wives went through a crisis of that kind. Dominique had advised her to get out of the house and to work: and once Jean-Charles had seen how much I earned he was all for it. Now there's no sort of reason for me to crack. I have as much work as I can do and people all round me: my life's happy. No, not the least danger. It's just a question of mood. I'm sure it often happens to the others too, and they don't make a song and dance about it. She turned round to the children. 'Did you have fun, poppets?'

'Oh, yes!' said Louise enthusiastically.

The smell of dead leaves came in through the open window, the stars were shining in the sort of sky she knew as a child, and all at once Laurence felt splendid.

The Ferrari passed them, with Dominique waving and her wispy scarf streaming in the wind: she really does have style. And Gilbert was extraordinary for fifty-six. A fine pair. Really she had been quite right to insist upon a clear-cut situation.

'They're well matched,' said Jean-Charles. 'For their age, a fine pair.'

A pair. Laurence looked attentively at Jean-Charles. She liked driving next to him. He was watching the road carefully, and she saw his profile, the profile that had stirred her so, ten years ago, and that moved her still. Seen from the front Jean-Charles was no longer quite the same—she no longer saw him in the same way. He had an intelligent and lively face, but it looked—what was the right word?—set, like all other faces. Seen from the side in the faint light the mouth seemed less decided, the eyes more dreamy. That was how she had seen him eleven years earlier, that was how she saw him when he was away, and sometimes, for the odd moment, when she was driving in the car next to him. They fell silent. The absence of words was like a secret agreement: it expressed an understanding too deep for speech. An illusion, perhaps. But as the car swallowed up the road and the children dozed in the back and Jean-Charles remained quiet, Laurence chose to believe in it.

All her anxiety had vanished when she settled herself at her table a little later: she was only rather tired, stupid with all that fresh air and ready to drift off in the way that Dominique used to cut very short—'Don't sit there day-dreaming: do something'—and that she now forbade on her own authority. 'I must hit upon this idea,' she said to herself, unscrewing her fountain-pen. What a pretty advertisement this would make, what a pretty picture promising—for the advantage of some furniture-dealer, shirtmaker or florist—security, happiness. The couple walking along the pavement by the parapet amidst the gentle murmur of the trees, gaze into the ideal home as they go by: under the standard lamp the man absorbed in his magazine, young and elegant in his angora pullover; the young woman sitting at her table, her pen in her hand; the harmony of the blacks, reds and yellows that match so well (such luck) with the yellows and reds of the dahlias. A little while ago, when I picked them, they were living flowers. Laurence thought of that king who turned everything he touched into gold and whose little daughter became a splendid metal doll. Everything she touched turned into a picture. *With wooden panelling you combine the elegance of town with all the poetry of the forest.* Through the leaves her eye caught the black run of the river: a ship went by, searching the banks with its white glare. The light splashed against the windows and suddenly it lit up a pair of entwined lovers: a picture of the past for me, who am the picture of their loving future, with the children whose existence they guess asleep in the bedrooms at the back. *The children made their way into a hollow tree and there they found themselves in an enchanting room all panelled in natural wood.* Follow up this idea.

She had always been a picture. Dominique had seen to that, Dominique whose childhood had been fascinated by pictures that were so different from her own life—a life that had been obstinately directed, with the whole of her intelligence and her immense energy, at filling the gap between the two. (You don't know what it is to have shoes with holes in them and to feel through your sock that you have walked on spit. You don't know what it is to see your friends with their hair beautifully washed nudging one another and sneering at you. No, you are not to go out with that mark on your skirt: go and change.) A faultless child, an accomplished adolescent, a perfect young woman. You were so clean-cut, so fresh, so perfect ... said Jean-Charles.

Everything was clear, fresh, perfect: the blue water in the swimming-pool, the opulent sound of the tennis-balls, the sharp white rock of the peaks, the rounded clouds in the smooth sky, the smell of the pines. Every morning when she opened her shutters Laurence gazed at a splendid glossy photograph. In the hotel garden the young men and the girls dressed in white, brown-skinned, polished by the sun like charming pebbles. And Laurence and Jean-Charles in white too, brown-skinned and polished. Suddenly one evening coming back from a drive his mouth on my mouth in the stopped car: the sudden blaze, the dizziness. Then for days and weeks on end I was not just a picture any more, but flesh and blood, longing and delight. And I also rediscovered that more secret happiness which I had known long before, sitting at my father's feet or holding his hand in mine ... Then once again, eighteen months ago, with Lucien: fire in my veins, the delicious liquefaction of my bones. She bit her lip. If Jean-Charles knew! In fact nothing had changed between Laurence and him. Lucien was peripheral. And besides he no longer stirs me as he used to.

'How's the idea coming along?'

'It'll come.'

The husband's attentive look; the young wife's pretty smile. She had often been told she had a pretty smile: she let it form on her lips. The idea would come. It always was hard to begin with—so many clichés that had been used before, so many traps to avoid. But she knew her job. I am not selling wooden panels: I am selling security, success and a touch of poetry into the bargain. When Dominique had suggested that she should make cut-out pictures she had succeeded so quickly and so completely that it looked like a natural vocation. Security. Wood is no more inflammable than stone or brick; put it without calling the notion of a fire to mind. That's where tact is wanted.

All at once she got up. Was Catherine crying tonight as well?

Louise was asleep. Catherine was gazing at the ceiling. Laurence bent over her. 'Not asleep, darling? What are you thinking about?'

'Nothing.'

Laurence kissed her, curious and puzzled. Mystery was not like Catherine: she was an open child—talkative, indeed. 'Everyone thinks about something. Try to tell me.'

Catherine hesitated for a moment: her mother's smile made up her mind for her. 'Mama, why do people live?'

That is exactly the sort of question children stun you with when all you are trying to do is to sell wooden panelling. Answer quickly.

'Sweetie, Papa and I would be very, very sad if you *weren't* alive.'

'But if you weren't alive either?'

Such anxiety in the eyes of this little girl I still treat as though she were a baby. Why does she ask herself this

20

question? So that is what is making her cry, then. 'This afternoon weren't you happy that you and I and everybody else was alive?'

'Yes.'

Catherine did not seem wholly convinced. Laurence had an inspiration. 'People are alive to make one another happy,' she said enthusiastically. She was quite proud of her reply.

With a wooden expression Catherine went on thinking, or rather she went on feeling for the right words. 'But what about the people who aren't happy: why are they alive?'

Here we are: we're coming to the heart of the matter. 'You've seen unhappy people? Where, darling?'

Catherine fell silent, with a frightened look. Where? Goya was cheerful, and she scarcely spoke any French. It was a rich neighbourhood: no tramps, no beggars: books, then? School friends?

'Are there girls at school who are unhappy?'

'Oh, no!'

Her voice seemed sincere. Louise was stirring in her bed and Catherine ought to be asleep; she obviously did not want to say any more and it would need time to bring her to it.

'I tell you what, we'll talk about it tomorrow. But if you know any unhappy people, we'll try and do something for them. You can treat sick people, give poor ones money—there are masses of things you can do.'

'Are there really? For everybody?'

'Dear me, I should cry all day long if there were people whose unhappiness couldn't be cured at all. Tell me all about it tomorrow. And I promise you we'll find something to be done. I promise,' she repeated, stroking Catherine's hair. 'Go to sleep now, darling.'

Catherine slipped down in her bed: she closed her eyes. Her mother's voice and kisses had calmed her. But what about tomorrow? As a rule Laurence never made thoughtless promises: and never had there been such a rash one as that.

Jean-Charles looked up.

'Catherine told me about a dream,' said Laurence. Tomorrow she would tell him the truth. Not this evening. Why? He was interested in the children. Laurence sat down and pretended to be absorbed in her search. Not this evening. He would produce five or six explanations straight off. She wanted to try to understand before he replied. What was it that was wrong? I cried too, at her age: how I cried! Perhaps that's why I never cry any more now. Mlle Houchet used to say, 'It will depend upon us whether these deaths were useless or not.' I believed her. She said so many things—be a man among men! She died of cancer. The exterminations; Hiroshima. In '45 there were reasons for a child of eleven to feel shattered. Indeed, Laurence had thought that all that horror for nothing was impossible; she had tried to believe in God, in another life where everything would be made up. Dominique had behaved beautifully: she had let her talk to a priest, and she had even chosen an intelligent one for her. In '45 that was natural enough. But nowadays if my ten-year-old daughter sobs, I'm the one who's at fault: Dominique and Jean-Charles would both blame me. She is capable of advising me to go and see a psychoanalyst. Catherine reads an immense amount —too much; and I don't really know what. I haven't the time. In any case the words would not have the same meaning for me as they have for her.

'Do you realize this? In our galaxy alone there are hundreds of inhabited planets!' said Jean-Charles, tapping his magazine with a thoughtful finger. 'We are like hens shut up in a chicken-run who take it for the whole world.'

'Oh, even on earth one is cooped up in such a narrow little circle.'

'Not nowadays. What with the papers, the television and presently the mundovision one lives on a planetary scale. The mistake is to suppose the planet is the universe. Still, by '85 the solar system will have been explored ... Doesn't that stir your imagination?'

'Frankly, no.'

'You don't possess any.'

I don't even know the people who live on the floor above, thought Laurence. She was very well informed about the neighbours on the other side of the party wall: their bath ran, their doors slammed, the radio poured forth songs and advertisements for Banania, the husband bawled out his wife, and after he had gone the wife bawled out their son. But what happened in the other three hundred and forty flats in the block? In the other houses in Paris? At Publinf she knew Lucien, Mona to a certain extent, and a few names and faces. Family: friends—a tiny closed circuit. And all these other equally inaccessible circuits. The world is always somewhere else; and there is no way of getting into it. Yet it has made its way into Catherine's life; it is frightening her and I ought to protect her from it. How can I get her to accept the fact that there are unhappy people? How can I get her to believe that they will stop being unhappy?

'Aren't you ready for bed?' asked Jean-Charles.

No idea was going to come that night and there was no point in trying to force it. She modelled her smile upon her husband's. 'I'm ready for bed.'

The evening rites, the cheerful sound of water in the bathroom, on the bed pyjamas smelling of lavender and Virginia tobacco, Jean-Charles smoking a cigarette while the shower washed Laurence clean of the cares of the day. Quickly she took off her make-up, put on her frail nightgown, and she was ready. (A splendid invention, the pill you swallow in the morning when you do your teeth: those horrid devices used to be so disagreeable.) In the coolness of the white sheets the nightgown slipped right back and then flew over her head: she gave herself up to tender nakedness. The happiness of making love. Violent pleasure, shot through with delight. After ten years of marriage, a perfect physical understanding. Yes; but one that did not change the colour of life. Love too was smooth, hygienic and habitual.

'Yes: your drawings are quite lovely,' said Laurence. Mona was really talented; she had invented a funny little character Laurence had often used in her campaigns—rather too often, said Lucien, who was the best motivation expert in the firm.

'But?' said Mona. She was rather like her character, intelligent, sharp and attractive.

'You know what Lucien says. One mustn't over-do humour. And in this case—wood's expensive; it's solemn, responsible stuff—a coloured photo gives the idea better.'

Laurence had kept two, taken according to her instructions: one in a timber-forest, with its moss, its mystery, the veiled, sumptuous gleam of the ancient trunks; and the other of a young woman in a misty déshabillé, smiling in the middle of a panelled room.

'I think they're punk,' said Mona.

'Punk, but they draw your attention.'

'I'll end up by getting the sack,' said Mona. 'Drawing doesn't mean anything any more in this joint. You people would always rather have photos.' She gathered up her sketches, and with curiosity in her voice she asked, 'What's happening with Lucien? Don't you see him any more?'

'Indeed I do.'

'You never ask me for an alibi now.'

'I'll be asking, all right.'

Mona went out of the office and Laurence returned to the polishing of the text that was to go with the picture. Her heart was not in it. 'Behold the lacerated state of the woman who goes out to work,' she said to herself ironically. (She used to feel far more lacerated when she did not have a job.) At home she tried to think up slogans. In the office she brooded about Catherine. For the last three days she had hardly thought of anything else.

The conversation had been long and muddled. Laurence wanted to know what book or what meeting had upset Catherine: what Catherine wanted to know was how unhappiness could be done away with. Laurence had talked about social workers who helped the old and the poor. About nurses and doctors who cured the sick.

'Can I be a doctor?'

'Certainly you can, if you go on working hard.'

Catherine's face lightened: they both of them talked about her future—she would look after children; their mothers too, but principally children.

'And what do you do for people who are unhappy?' The pitiless gaze of children who are not playing at any sort of game at all.

'I help Papa earn our living. It's because of me that you will be able to go on with your education and cure the sick.'

'And Papa?'

'He builds houses for people who havent got any. That's also a way of helping them, you see.' (Horrible lie. But what truth could she turn to?) Catherine was still puzzled. Why wasn't everybody given enough to eat? Laurence started asking questions again and in the end the child spoke about the poster. Because the poster was really important, or to hide something else?

Maybe after all the poster was the true explanation. The power of the image. 'Two thirds of the world goes hungry,' and that child's face, that beautiful face with its eyes too big and its mouth closed upon a terrible secret. In my eyes that poster is a sign—a sign that the struggle against hunger is going on. In Catherine's it is a little boy of her own age who is hungry. I remember: how insensitive the grown-ups seemed to me! There are so many things we don't notice; or rather we do notice them but we go right on because we know there's no point in stopping. What's the use of a guilty conscience? And on this point Papa and Jean-Charles are in agreement for once. That business of the tortures, three years ago—I made myself ill over it, or very nearly: and what did that accomplish? You're obliged to get used to the horrors of this world, there are too many of them. The cramming of geese, excision, lynching, abortions, suicides, brutally ill-treated children, death-camps, the slaughter of hostages, repression: you see it all on the cinema or on the television and you ignore it. It must inevitably vanish; it's only a question of time. But children live in the present: they have no defence. 'They ought to think of the children. They ought never to stick pictures like that up on the walls,' said Laurence to herself. An abject thought. Abject: a great word of mine when I was fifteen. But what does it mean? Mine is the normal reaction of a woman trying to protect her daughter.

'This evening Papa will explain everything,' Laurence ended up by saying. Ten and a half: the time for a daughter to move a little way from her mother and to attach herself to her father. And he'll find persuasive arguments better than I can, she thought.

To begin with Jean-Charles' tone had embarrased her. Not exactly ironic, nor yet condescending—paternalistic. Then he had delivered a very clear, very convincing little speech: up until now the different parts of the world had been a great way from one another; people had not been very good at managing and they were selfish. That poster proved that we wanted things to change. Nowadays it was possible to produce more food than before and to carry it quickly and easily from the rich countries to the poor ones: there were organizations that were seeing to it. Jean-Charles grew lyrical, as he did every time he summoned up the future: the deserts were covered with wheat, vegetables and fruit; all lands had become the Promised Land; all children, stuffed with rice, tomatoes and oranges, beamed with delight. Catherine listened, fascinated: she could see the orchards and the waving fields.

'No one will be unhappy any more, in ten years' time?'

'I can't say that. But everybody will have enough to

eat; and everybody will be much happier.'

Then in a voice full of conviction she said, 'I would much rather have been born ten years later.'

Jean-Charles laughed, proud of his daughter's forwardness. He was satisfied with the way she was getting on at school, and he did not take her tears seriously. Children were often rather lost when they began in the upper school; but as for Catherine, she thought Latin a game and she had good reports in all her subjects. 'She'll really get somewhere,' Jean-Charles told me. But for the moment she's a child with a heavy heart, and I don't know how to comfort her.

The office telephone rang. 'Laurence? Are you alone?' 'Yes.' 'I'll come and say how do you do.' He's going to be cross, thought Laurence: it's quite true that I have neglected him since the end of the holidays; I had to open up the house and get Goya used to running it; and Louise had bronchitis. It was eighteen months now since the party at Publinf—the party from which custom barred both husbands and wives. They had danced together a great deal (he danced very well), they had kissed, and the miracle had happened again—that fire in her veins, that dizziness. They had ended up at his place and she had not gone home until dawn: she pretended that she had been drunk—although she had not touched a single drink: she never drank at all—and she felt no sort of remorse because Jean-Charles would know nothing about it and because it was not going to go on. Then what turmoil of spirit! He pursued me, he wept, I gave way, he broke off, I went through hell, I looked for the red Alfa Romeo everywhere, I sat glued to the telephone, he came back, 'leave your husband' he begged, no never but I love you, he insulted me, he broke off again, I wanted, I hoped, I lost hope, we came together once more, what happiness, I've suffered so much without you, and I without you, 'tell your husband everything', never—All these comings and goings and always back at the same place . . .

'I was just wanting your advice,' said Laurence. 'Which of these two roughs do you prefer?'

Lucien leant over her shoulder. He looked closely at the two photos: she was touched by his thoughtful air.

'Hard to say. They work on utterly different motivations.'

'Which works best?'

'I don't know any convincing statistics. Trust in your hunch.' He laid his hand on Laurence's shoulder. 'When are we going to have dinner together?'

'Jean-Charles is going to the Roussillon with Vergne in a week's time.'

'A week!'

'Be understanding. I'm having a worrying time at home: because of my daughter.'

'I can't see what that has to do with it.'

'I can.'

The too-familiar argument: you don't want to see me any more, of course I do, do try to understand, I understand only too well ... (Was there some other spot in the galaxy with another Lucien and another Laurence saying just the same things to one another? It was certainly the case in offices, rooms and cafés in Paris, London, Rome, New York, Tokyo and perhaps even Moscow.)

'Let's have a drink together tomorrow evening after the office? All right?'

He looked at her reproachfully. 'I have no choice.'

He went away cross: a pity. He had made a real effort to accept the situation. He knew that she would never divorce and he no longer threatened to break things off. She was very fond of him: he was a rest from Jean-Charles—so unlike: water and fire. He liked novels with a story; he liked childhood memories, asking questions, strolling about the streets. And then when he looked at her she felt precious. Precious: she let herself be taken in, too. You think you are very fond of a man: in fact you value a certain notion of yourself, an illusion of freedom or of the unforeseen—mirages. (Is that really true, or is my job distorting my attitude?) She finished writing her copy. In the end she chose the young woman in the filmy déshabillé. She closed her office and got into her car: while she was putting on her gloves and changing her shoes cheerfulness bubbled up inside her. In her imagination she was already in the flat in the rue de l'Université, crammed with books and smelling strongly of tobacco. Unfortunately she never stayed there long. It was her father she loved best—best in the world—and she saw much more of Dominique. My whole life has been like that: it was my father I loved and my mother who formed me.

'You vile beast!' She had hesitated half a second too long and the fat brute had whipped into the place in front of her. Round and round again in these little one-way streets with cars bumper to bumper on either side. Underground car-parks, urban centres on four levels, a technical city under the bed of the Seine: in ten years' time. I too would rather be living ten years later. A place at last! She walked a hundred yards, and she was in another world: the traditional concierge's lodge with its pleated curtain and the smell of cooking, then a silent courtyard, a stone staircase and the echo of your feet as you walk up it.

'It's becoming more and more impossible to park.'

'You take the words right out of my mouth.'

With her father even trivialities were no longer trivial, because of the collusive gleam in his eye. They both of them loved complicity—those moments when two people are so close that they might be living for one another alone. After he had sat her down and given her a glass of orange-juice, the mischievous gleam reappeared as he asked, 'How is your mother?'

'In great form.'

'Who is she copying at present?'

It was an old gag between them, this question of Freud's about an hysteric. The fact was that Dominique was always imitating somebody.

'I think at present it's Jacqueline Verdelet. She has the same hair-do and she's abandoned Cardin for Balenciaga.'

'She sees the Verdelets? That riff-raff ... It's true that she's never minded what kind of a hand she shakes ... Did you speak to her about Serge?'

'She won't do anything for him.'

'I thought as much.'

'It doesn't seem that she's really very passionately attached to my uncle and aunt. She calls them Darby and Joan.'

'Not particularly apt. I think my sister has lost a great many illusions about Bernard. She's not in love with him any more.'

'What about him?'

'He's never valued her at her true worth.'

To be in love: true worth. For him these words had a meaning. He had been in love with Dominique. And with whom apart from her? Was there any other woman who had been worthy of being loved by him? Surely not; otherwise there would not be that disillusioned line at the corner of his mouth.

'People never cease astonishing me,' he went on. 'Bernard is opposed to the régime and yet he thinks it perfectly normal that his son should want to get into the ORTF, which is a government domain. I must be a hopeless old idealist—I've always tried to make my life coincide with my principles.'

'Personally I don't have any principles,' said Laurence sadly.

'You don't wave them about, but you are straight, which is far better than the other thing,' said her father warmly.

She laughed and sipped her orange-juice: she felt fine. What was there she would not give for praise from him? He was incapable of a low compromise or scheme and he was indifferent to money—unique.

He searched among his gramophone-records. No hi-fi system: only a great many lovingly-chosen discs. 'I'm going to play you something very fine, a new recording of *L'Incoronazione di Poppea*.'

Laurence tried to concentrate. A woman was saying farewell to her country and her friends. It was beautiful. She looked at her father: oh to be able to sink into oneself like that. He alone possessed what she thought she had found in Jean-Charles and Lucien: upon his face there was a reflection of the infinite. To be delightful company for oneself: to be a hearth that sends out warmth. I indulge in the luxury of remorse: I blame myself for my neglect: but it is I who need him. She looked at her father; she wondered where his secret lay and whether she would ever be able to discover it. She did not listen. For a long while now music had no longer said anything to her. Monteverdi's pathos, the tragic utterances of Beethoven, referred to pains of a kind that she had never felt—huge, vehement, mastered pains. She had experienced a piercing anguish now and then, a certain wretchedness of mind, forlornness, perturbation, emptiness, boredom—above all boredom. No one celebrates boredom in music.

'Yes, it's perfectly splendid,' she said fervently. (Say what you think, said Mlle Houchet. Even with her father it was impossible. You say what people expect you to say.)

'I knew you'd like it. Shall I put on the rest?'

'Not today. I want to ask your advice. About Catherine.'

At once he was listening attentively, taking in what she said, not knowing the answer beforehand. When she had finished he thought for a while. 'Everything is all right between Jean-Charles and you?'

Very much to the point. Maybe I should not have wept so over the murdered Jewish children if there had not been such brooding silences at home.

'Perfect.'

'You answer very quickly.'

'It's quite true, everything is fine. I don't possess his energy, but that cancels out and balances things for the children. Unless I'm too absent-minded.'

'Because of your work.'

'No. I have the feeling that I'm absent-minded in general. But not with the children: no, I don't think so.'

Her father said nothing. 'What answer can I give Catherine?' she said.

'There's no answer to give. Once the question has been asked, there's nothing you can reply.'

'But I must reply. Why does one exist? All right, that's abstract, that's metaphysics—I'm not too worried by that question. But unhappiness: that's terribly wounding for a child.'

'Even through unhappiness joy can be found. But I admit that it's not easy to convince a ten-year-old girl of that.'

'Well then?'

'Well then, I will try to talk to her and come to understand what's worrying her. Then I'll tell you.'

Laurence stood up. 'I must go: it's time.'

Maybe Papa will be cleverer than Jean-Charles or me: he knows how to talk to children—he hits the right tone with everyone. And he thinks up delightful presents. When he arrived at the flat he took a cardboard cylinder out of his pocket, a thing like an immense sugar stick, with brilliant stripes. They each put an eye to one end of it in turn: Louise, Catherine and Laurence: a wonderland of colours and shapes that formed, fell apart, quivered with light and multiplied in fleeting symmetry within an octagon. A kaleidoscope with nothing inside: it was the outer world that furnished its material—the dahlias, the carpet, the curtains, the books. Jean-Charles looked through it too. 'It would be extraordinarily useful to a person who designed wall-paper, or cloth,' he said. 'Ten ideas a minute . . .'

Laurence served the soup, and her father spooned it down without comment. ('You don't *eat*,' he said to her once. 'You absorb nourishment.' She cared as little as

Jean-Charles for the pleasures of the table.) He told the children stories that made them laugh, and without seeming to ask questions he sounded them. Take the moon: it would be fun to walk about on it—would they be afraid of going there? No, not at all; if they went that would be because it could be done—it would be no more dangerous than taking a plane. That man in space had not astonished them in the least; indeed, on the television they had thought him rather a clot; they had read the story before in comic strips—what was more they had read one about a landing on the moon, and the only thing that surprised them was that no one had got there yet. They would very much like to know the men, the super-men and the sub-men their father talked about, who lived on other planets. They described them, they interrupted one another, excited by the sound of their own voices, their grandfather's presence and the comparative splendour of the meal. Did they do astronomy at the lycée? No. But they had fun, said Louise. Catherine talked about her friend Brigette, who was a year older than she and so intelligent, and about her French mistress, who was rather stupid. Stupid in what way? She said stupid things. There was nothing more to be got out of her. As they stuffed themselves with pineapple ice they begged their grandfather to take them for a drive one Sunday as he had promised. The châteaux of the Loire, the ones they talked about in French history...

'Don't you think that Laurence is worrying over nothing?' asked Jean-Charles when the three of them were alone. 'At Catherine's age all intelligent children ask themselves questions.'

'But why those particular questions?' said Laurence. 'She leads a very sheltered life.'

'What life is sheltered nowadays, with the papers, the television and the films?' asked her father.

'As for television, I do take great care,' said Laurence. 'And we don't leave newspapers lying around.' She had forbidden Catherine to read the papers: she had explained, with examples, that when one does not know very much there is the danger of getting things wrong; and she had explained that newspapers often lied.

'Still, you can't oversee everything. Do you know her new friend?'

'No.'

'Tell her to bring her. Try to find out what she and Catherine talk about.'

'At all events Catherine is cheerful and healthy, and she works well,' said Jean-Charles. 'There's no need to wring one's hands over a little fit of over-sensitivity.'

Laurence wanted to think that Jean-Charles was right. When she went to kiss them goodnight the children were bounding about on their beds and shrieking with laughter. She laughed too and tucked them in. But she remembered Catherine's anxious face. Who is Brigitte? Even if she plays no part in all this I ought to have asked. There are too many things I don't think of.

She went back to the living-room. Her father and Jean-Charles were engaged in one of those arguments they had every Wednesday.

'No, no, men have not lost their roots at all,' said Jean-Charles impatiently. 'What is new is that they are rooted on the scale of the planet.'

'They no longer belong anywhere, although they are to be found in every corner. Never have people been so bad at travelling.'

'You want a journey to be a complete change of scene. But the world is only one country now. So much so that one is astonished because moving from one place to another still requires the passage of time.' He looked at Laurence. 'You remember the last time we came back from New York? We were so used to jets that seven hours of flying seemed to us to last for ever.'

'Proust says the same thing about the telephone. Don't you recall? It is where he rings up his grandmother from Doncières. He says that he has grown so used to the miracle of this voice at a distance that waiting for his call

34

to be put through vexes him.'

'I don't remember,' said Jean-Charles.

'The children of this generation think it perfectly natural that men should walk about in space. Nothing amazes anybody any more. Presently we shall look upon technical achievement as nature itself and we shall live in a totally inhuman world.'

'Why inhuman? Man's aspect will alter: he can't be imprisoned in one rigid, unchanging concept. But leisure will allow him to rediscover those values you prize so highly—individuality, art...'

'Things are not developing in that direction.'

'Oh yes they are! Take decorative art, take architecture. People are no longer satisfied with the functional. There is a return to baroque of a sort, that is to say to aesthetic values.'

What's the good? thought Laurence. In any case time will run no faster and no slower. Jean-Charles is already living in 1985 and Papa is looking back sadly to 1925. At least he talks about a world that did exist and that he loved: Jean-Charles invents a future that may never come into being at all.

'You must admit that there is nothing on earth as ugly as the old-fashioned railway landscape,' he said. 'Nowadays the railways and the electricity board are making a remarkable effort to preserve the beauty of the French countryside.'

'A pretty disastrous effort.'

'Not at all.' Jean-Charles produced a list of stations and powerhouses that matched their surroundings perfectly. It was always Jean-Charles who had the better of these arguments; he could quote facts. Laurence smiled at her father. He had taken refuge in silence, but the gleam in his eye and the set of his mouth showed that his convictions were intact.

He will be going in a minute, thought Laurence, and once more I shall not have made anything like the most of his being here. What's the matter with me? My mind always drifts off to other things.

'Your father is a perfect example of the man who refuses to enter the twentieth century,' said Jean-Charles an hour later.

'As for you, you live in the twenty-first,' said Laurence, smiling.

She settled at her table. She had to go carefully through the recent survey in depth that Lucien had conducted: she opened the file. It was wearisome: indeed, it was depressing. Smoothness, brilliance, shine; the dream of gliding, of icy perfection; erotic values and infantile values (innocence); speed, domination, warmth, security. Was it possible that all tastes could be explained by such primitive phantasms? Scarcely likely. It was a thankless kind of task these psychologists carried out: countless questionnaires, subtleties and refinements, and the same answers came up every time. People wanted novelty, but with no risk; they wanted products to be exciting and yet of solid, sober quality, of high prestige value, but low price ... She was always faced with the same problem—how to excite curiosity, to astonish and at the same time to reassure: behold the magic product that will completely change our lives without putting us out in the very least.

'Did you ask yourself a great many questions when you were little?' she asked.

'I imagine so.'

'You don't remember what?'

'No.' He sank back into his book. He claimed to have forgotten everything about his childhood. Father, a small manufacturer in Normandy: two brothers: normal relationships with his mother: no sort of reason for escaping from his past. Yet in fact he never spoke of it.

He was reading. Since she found this file so dreary she might read too. Read what? Jean-Charles loved books that talked about nothing. You know, what's so terrific about these young writers is that they don't write to tell a story: they write to write, as you might pile up stones one on top of the other, for the pleasure of it. She had begun a description, in three hundred pages, of a suspension-bridge: she had not been able to hold out ten minutes. As for the novels that Lucien recommended, they talked about people and events as far removed from her own life as Monteverdi.

So all right. Books don't say anything to me any more. But I ought to try to be better informed: I've grown so ignorant. Papa used to say, 'Laurence will be a bookworm, like me.' And instead of that ... She quite understood why she had gone back during the first years of her marriage—it was perfectly usual. Love and motherhood constitute a violent emotional shock when you marry young and when a settled balance has not yet grown up between the intellectual and emotional aspects of your personality. It seemed to me that I had no future any more: Jean-Charles and the children had one, not me; so what was the point of keeping myself up to scratch? A vicious circle: I let myself go, I grew bored and I felt myself less and less a creature in my own personal possession. (And of course her nervous breakdown had had deeper causes; but she had not needed analysis to come out of it: she had taken a job that interested her and she had recovered.) And now? It is quite another problem. I lack time, and the necessity of finding ideas and writing slogans is growing into an obsession. Still, at least she used to read the papers for some time after she had joined Publinf: now she relied upon Jean-Charles to keep her in touch. It was not good enough. 'Form your own opinion!' said Mlle Houchet. How disappointed she would be if she could see me today! Laurence reached out for *Le Monde*, lying there on a low table. Discouraging: you ought never to lose the thread, otherwise you are all at sea. Everything always began some time ago. Where was Burundi? What was the OCAM? Why were the Buddhist monks demonstrating? Who was General Delgado? Just where did Ghana lie on the map? She folded up the paper; but still she was rather comforted, for there was no telling what you might find in it. It's all very well for me to armour myself: I'm not as resistant as they are. 'The convulsive aspect of women,' says Jean-Charles, although he is a feminist. I struggle against it: I utterly loathe being convulsive, so the best thing to do is to avoid any occasion for it.

She picked up the file again. Why does one exist? That's not my problem. One does exist. The thing to do is to take no notice but go at it with a run and to keep on going right on until you die. My impetus was broken five years ago. I set off again. But how time drags. You relapse. My problem is that occasional caving-in, those spaced-out collapses, as though there existed an answer to Catherine's question, a terrifying answer. Nonsense! It's slipping towards neurosis to think that. I shall not relapse. Now I am quite aware of the real reasons for my breakdown and I have gone beyond them: I have brought the conflict between my feelings for Jean-Charles and my feelings for my father out into the open and it does not torment me any longer. I have settled accounts with myself.

The children were asleep; Jean-Charles was reading. Somewhere Lucien was thinking of her. She felt her life around her, full, warm, a nest, a cocoon; and all that was needed was a little care to prevent anything breaking in upon this security.

CHAPTER 2

'Why does Gilbert want to see me?' Set back in their
damp gardens that smelt of autumn and the provinces,
all these houses in Neuilly were like so many nursing-
homes. 'Don't tell Dominique.' There had been fear in
his voice. Cancer? Or perhaps heart?

'Thank you for coming.'

Harmonizing greys and reds; black carpet; rare editions on lovely bookshelves; two modern pictures with
expensive signatures; the hi-fi system; the bar: her job
consisted of selling this millionaire's study to each
customer for the price of an odd length of rep or a white-
wood whatnot.

'A drop of whisky?'

'No thanks.' Her throat was dry. 'What's the matter?'

'Fruit juice?'

'All right.'

He poured some out for her, he poured some out for
himself, he put ice-cubes in the glass; he took his time.
Because he's used to taking things at his own pace and
speaking only when he chooses? Or is he in fact embarrassed?

'You know Dominique well. You can advise me.'

Either heart or cancer. It must be serious for Gilbert to
ask Laurence's advice. She heard the words that hung up
there in the air, devoid of meaning. 'I'm in love with a
girl.'

'How do you mean?'

'In love: you know, love. With a girl of nineteen.'

There was the beginning of a fat smile on his mouth as
he spoke in a fatherly tone, as if he were explaining a
very simple fact to a backward child. 'It's by no means
unusual nowadays for a girl of nineteen to love a man of

39

over fifty.'

'So she loves you too?'

'Yes.'

No, cried Laurence silently. Mama! My poor Mama! She would not question Gilbert: she would not help him get it out. He remained silent. She gave way: she was not of his calibre.

'Well then?'

'Well then we are going to be married.'

This time she cried out loud, 'But that's impossible!'

'Marie-Claire agrees to the divorce. She knows Patricia and she's very fond of her.'

'Patricia?'

'Yes. Lucile de Saint-Chamont's daughter.'

'It's impossible!' said Laurence again. She had seen Patricia once, a blonde, affected twelve-year-old; and last year her photograph, all in white at the debs' ball: a ravishing little penniless goose whom her mother was throwing into the wealthiest lap she could find. 'You're not going to leave Dominique? Seven years!'

'Precisely.' He had put on his cynical voice and his mouth was pouting into a smile. He was plainly and simply a cad. Laurence felt her heart beating very hard, very fast: she was living in one of those nightmares where you do not know whether things are really happening to you or whether you are at a horror film. Marie-Claire agreed to a divorce: of course she would be only too delighted to play a dirty trick on Dominique.

'But Dominique loves you. She thinks you are going to finish your life together. She will never be able to bear being deserted.'

'You bear things, you know,' said Gilbert. 'You bear them.'

Laurence was silent. Words were useless, she knew.

'Come, don't look so aghast. Your mother is resilient. She's perfectly aware that a woman of fifty-one is older than a man of fifty-six. She's very much attached to her career and her social life: she'll make the rest of it. I'm only wondering—and that's what I wanted to ask you about—what is the best way of breaking it to her.'

'Any way is bad.'

Gilbert looked at Laurence with that enchanted air that had earned him his reputation as a charmer. 'I have a great deal of confidence in your judgment. Do you think I should just tell her that I don't love her any more, or should I speak about Patricia right away?'

'Oh don't do that!' begged Laurence. 'She couldn't bear it.'

'I shall speak to her tomorrow afternoon. Manage things so that you see her in the evening. She'll need someone. Telephone me afterwards and let me know how she has taken it.'

'No I shan't,' said Laurence.

'The thing is to hurt her as little as possible; indeed, I should like to be able to keep her friendship—it's for her own good.'

Laurence stood up and walked towards the door. He took her arm. 'Don't tell her about this conversation.'

'I shall do what I choose.'

Gilbert mumbled banalities behind her: she did not give him her hand: she slammed the door: she hated him. It was a relief to be able to admit it to herself all at once—'I always loathed Gilbert.' Her feet crushed the dead leaves as she walked and all round her there was fear, as thick as a fog; but one hard clear fact shone through the murk: 'I hate him!' And she thought, 'Dominique will hate him!' Dominique was proud: she was strong. 'You don't behave like a shop-girl.' She would suffer, but her pride would save her. The woman who stands up to a break—who takes it with style: a difficult role, but a fine one. She will fling herself into work, take a new lover ... Suppose I were to go and warn her, right away? Laurence sat there motionless at the wheel of her car. Suddenly she was sweating and she felt like being sick. Impossible that Dominique should hear the words Gilbert meant to say to her. Something would happen:

he would die in the night or she would. Or the world would come to an end.

Tomorrow was today: the world had not come to an end. Laurence parked on a pedestrian crossing: damn the summons. Three times she had telephoned from the office and each time there had been the engaged sound. Dominique had unhooked the receiver. She took the lift; she wiped her moist hands. Try to look natural.

'I'm not disturbing you? I couldn't get you on the phone and I wanted to ask your advice.' It was terribly obvious, for she never asked her mother for advice; but Dominique had scarcely taken any notice. 'Come in,' she said.

They sat down in the 'silence/rest area' of the big discreet, muted drawing-room. In a vase there was a huge bunch of spiky yellow flowers that looked like evil birds. Dominique's eyes were swollen. Had she been crying, then? In a voice of almost triumphant challenge she said, 'I've something terrific to tell you!'

'What?'

'Gilbert has just told me he loves another woman.'

'It's a joke! Who?'

'He didn't tell me. He only said we had to "set our relationship on another footing". A sweet phrase! He won't come to Feuverolles this week-end.' The bantering voice trembled with fury. 'He's ditching me! But I'll find out who she is and I promise you I won't do her any sort of good!'

Laurence hesitated: get it over with right away? Her heart failed her: she was afraid. Gain time 'It's just a passing thing, I'm sure.'

'Gilbert never has them: he only has full-blown desires.' A sudden yell: 'The swine! The swine!'

Laurence seized her mother by the shoulders. 'Don't shout.'

'I'll shout as much as I like. Swine, swine!'

Laurence would never have believed that her mother

was capable of shouting like this, that shouts like this could be uttered: it was like bad melodrama. On the stage, fine; but not genuine cries, not in real life. The harsh voice soared, indecent in the insipidity of the silence/rest area: 'Swine! Swine!'

(In another drawing-room, wholly different and exactly the same, with vases full of expensive flowers, the same cry was coming out of another mouth: 'The swine!')

Dominique collapsed on the divan. 'Just imagine it,' she sobbed. 'Doing such a thing to me. He's ditching me like a shop-girl.'

'You didn't suspect anything?'

'Nothing. He took me in completely. You saw him the other Sunday—he was all smiles.'

'What did he say exactly?'

Dominique sat up. She ran her fingers through her hair: the tears were streaming down her face. 'That he owed me the truth. That he had the highest opinion of me, he admired me: the usual crap. But he loved someone else.'

'You didn't ask her name?'

'I set about it badly,' muttered Dominique. She wiped her eyes. 'I can just hear them, all my dear loving friends. Gilbert Mortier has chucked Dominique. How delighted they'll be!'

'Replace him right away: there are plenty of men who run after you.'

'Look at them—nasty little climbers...'

'Travel. Go off somewhere: show them you can do without him. He's a swine, you're perfectly right. Do your best to forget him.'

'He'd be charmed! Don't you see how that would suit him?' She stood up: she walked to and fro, across the drawing-room. 'I'll get him back. By hook or by crook.' She gave Laurence a savage look. 'He was my last chance, don't you understand?'

'Oh, no.'

43

'Of course he was. At fifty-one you don't remake your life.' In an obsessed voice she repeated, 'I'll get him back! By fair means or foul.'

'Foul?'

'If I find a way of bringing pressure to bear on him.'

'What way?'

'I'll see.'

'But what would be the point of keeping him, if it was against his will?'

'Keeping him would be the point. I won't be a jilted woman.'

She sat down again, with her eyes set and her mouth closed tight. Laurence talked. She said words she had heard from her mother long ago—dignity, calmness, courage, self-respect, facing up to things, behaving with style, playing the handsome part. Dominique made no reply. Wearily she said, 'Go home. I have to think. Be kind and telephone the Pétridès for me and say I have a sore throat.'

'Will you be able to sleep?'

'At all events I shan't overdo the barbiturates, if that's what's worrying you.'

She took Laurence's hands in an unusual, embarrassing gesture: her fingers tightened on her wrists. 'Try to find out who that woman is.'

'I don't know Gilbert's set.'

'Try, nevertheless.'

Laurence walked slowly down the stairs. There was something knotted in her chest that prevented her from breathing. She would have liked to melt with tenderness and sorrow. But there was still that cry in her ears; she could still see that wicked look. Fury and wounded vanity, a pain as agonizing as the heartbreak of love: but with no love in it. Who could love Gilbert, really love him? And as for Dominique, had she ever loved? Could she love? (He walked up and down the house like a soul in torment: he had loved her; he loved her still. And Laurence melted with tenderness and sorrow. And since

44

then there had always been a kind of baleful aura about Dominique.) Even her suffering did not make her human. It was as though one heard the grating of crayfish, an unformed sound that evoked nothing, nothing except maybe naked pain. Far more unbearable than if one could share it.

I tried not to hear, but the crayfish were still grating in my ears when I reached home. Louise was whipping eggwhite in the kitchen under Goya's eye: I kissed her. 'Is Catherine back?' 'She's in her room, with Brigitte.' They were sitting there opposite one another, in the dark. I switched on the light. Brigitte got up. *'Bonjour m'dame.'* Straight away I noticed the big safety-pin stuck in the hem of her skirt—a child without a mother, Catherine had told me. Tall, thin, brown hair cut very short and rather dirty, a faded blue pullover: better cared for she might look pretty. The room was in a mess—chairs upside-down, cushions on the floor.

'I'm very glad to see you.' I kissed Catherine. 'What are you playing at?'

'We are talking.'

'But all this mess?'

'Oh, we and Louise were fooling about a little while ago.'

'We'll tidy everything,' said Brigitte.

'There's no hurry.'

I turned an armchair the right way up and sat down. I didn't in the least mind their racing round, jumping over the furniture and knocking it over; but what had they been talking about when I came in?

'What were you talking about?'

'Oh, we were just talking,' said Catherine.

Standing there Brigitte examined me, not brazenly but with open curiosity. I was somewhat embarrassed. Grown-ups never really look at one another. Those eyes were seeing me. On the table there was the *Don Quixote*—a shortened, illustrated version—that Catherine had lent her friend. I picked it up. 'Have you finished it? Did you like it? Do sit down.'

She sat down. 'I didn't finish it.' She gave me a very pretty smile—not a child's smile at all and indeed somewhat coquettish. 'I get bored when a book is too long. And then I like true stories.'

'Historical things?'

'Yes. And travels; and what you read in the papers.'

'Does your Papa let you read the papers?'

She looked taken aback, confused; in a hesitant voice she murmured, 'Yes.'

Papa was right, I thought; I don't supervise everything. If she brings newspapers to school, if she tells what she has read in them . . . all those horrible police-court items, wickedly ill-treated children, children drowned by their own mothers . . . 'Do you understand it all?'

'My brother explains.'

Her brother was a student, her father a doctor. Alone with these two men. Not much supervision, for sure. Lucien says that girls who have big brothers mature faster than others: perhaps that is why she already has the ways of a little woman.

'What do you want to do in life? Have you made plans?'

They looked at one another with a conspiratorial air. 'I'm going to be a doctor,' said Catherine. 'She's going to be an agricultural expert.'

'An agricultural expert? Do you like the country?'

'My grandfather says the future depends on agricultural experts.'

I did not like to ask who this grandfather was. I looked at my watch. Quarter to eight. 'Catherine has to go and get ready for dinner. I expect they are waiting for you too, at home.'

'Oh, we eat when we like in my house,' she said in an offhand tone. 'I don't suppose there's anybody there yet.'

Yes, her condition was plain enough—a neglected child who had learnt to fend for herself. She was neither allowed nor forbidden to do anything: she was growing up just as chance would have it. How childish Catherine seemed next to her! It would have been kind to keep her for dinner. But Jean-Charles loathes anything unexpected. And I don't know why, but I did not particularly want him to meet Brigitte.

'Still, it's time you went home. But wait a moment— I'll put a stitch in your skirt.'

Her ears suddenly went fiery red. 'Oh, please don't bother.'

'Yes: it's ugly.'

'I'll mend it as soon as I get back.'

'Let me fix the pin, anyhow.'

I did so, and she smiled. 'How kind you are!'

'It would be nice if we got to know one another a little better. Would you care to come to the Musée de l'Homme with Catherine and Louise on Thursday?'

'Oh, yes please.'

Catherine took Brigitte as far as the front door: they whispered and giggled. I should have liked to sit in the dark with a little girl of my own age, giggling and whispering. But Dominique always used to say, 'No doubt your friend is very nice; but my poor darling, how dreadfully commonplace she is.' Marthe had a friend, the daughter of one of Papa's friends, a dull, stupid girl. Not me. Ever.

'She's very nice, your friend.'

'We have fun together.'

'Does she get good marks?'

'Oh yes, she's always top.'

'Yours aren't as good as they were at the beginning of the month. You're feeling all right?'

'Yes.'

I did not press it. 'She's older than you: that's why they allow her to read newspapers. But you remember what I told you: you're too young.'

'I remember.'

'And you don't disobey?'

'No.' There were reservations in her voice

'You don't seem very sure of it.'

'I am, though. Only it's not hard to understand what Brigitte tells me, you know.'

I felt at a loss. I liked Brigitte. But was she having a good influence upon Catherine?

'It's odd to want to be an agricultural expert. Do you understand that?'

'I'd rather be a doctor. I'm going to cure the sick and she'll make wheat and tomatoes grow in the desert and everyone will have enough to eat.'

'Did you show her the poster with the hungry little boy?'

'It was she who showed it to me.'

Obviously. I sent her to wash her hands and brush her hair and went into Louise's room. She was sitting at her desk drawing. Memory came back to me: the dark room with a single small lamp lit, the coloured crayons, a long day spangled with little delights behind me, and outside the world, vast and mysterious. Precious moments lost for ever. They would be lost for ever for them too one day. The pity of it! Stop them growing up. Or else ... what?

'What a pretty drawing, sweetheart.'

'There. It's a present.'

'Thank you. I'll put it on the table. Did you have a good time with Brigitte?'

'She taught me some dances ...' Louise's voice grew sad. 'But afterwards they sent me out of the room.'

'They had things to talk about. And then that way you could help Goya get dinner ready. Papa will be proud when he knows that it was practically you that made the soufflé.'

She laughed; then we heard the key in the lock and she ran to meet her father.

That was yesterday. And Laurence's mind dwelt upon it. She saw Brigitte's smile again—'How kind you are'— and her heart melted. This friendship might be a good thing for Catherine; she was old enough to take an interest in what was happening in the world. I don't talk to her enough myself and she's shy of her father; only she must not have any traumatic experiences either. Brigette's maternal grandparents live in Israel: she spent last year with them, and it was that which kept her back at school. Had there been deaths in her family? Had she told Catherine about all those horrors that used to make me weep so? I must watch out; I must keep in touch; I must find out about my daughter. Laurence tried to concentrate upon *France-Soir*. Still another ghastly newsitem. Twelve years old: hanged himself in prison. Asked for bananas and a towel, and hanged himself. 'Incidental expenses.' Gilbert explained that there were necessarily incidental expenses in every community. Yes, necessarily. But for all that this story would utterly horrify Catherine.

Gilbert. 'In love: you know, love.' What a swine! 'Swine, swine!' shrieked Dominique in the silence/rest area. This morning on the telephone she said in a brooding voice that she had slept well, and she hung up very quickly. What can I do for her? Nothing. It is so rare that one can do anything for anybody ... For Catherine, yes. Let's do it, then. Know how to answer her questions and even anticipate them. Bring her to the discovery of reality without frightening her. To do that I first have to have information. Jean-Charles reproaches me for not taking any interest in my own century: ask him to tell me what books to read: make myself read them. This was not a new plan after all. From time to time Laurence made resolutions but without really intending to keep them. (Why, in point of fact?) This time it was different. It was a question of Catherine. She would never forgive herself if she were to fail.

'It's lovely, your being here,' said Lucien.

Laurence, in a dressing-gown, was sitting in a leather armchair, and he, also in a dressing-gown, was at her feet, his face lifted towards her.

'I love it, too.'

'I wish you were here for ever.'

They had made love, eaten a little dinner, gossiped for a while, and made love again. She liked being in this room: there was a divan covered with a skin, a table, two black leather armchairs bought at the second-hand market, on the shelves a few books, an astronomical telescope, a compass and a sextant; skis and pigskin suitcases in a corner; it was casual, nothing luxurious about it; but it was not surprising that the wardrobe contained such quantities of well-cut suits, suède jackets, cashmere pullovers, silk scarves, shoes. Lucien slipped open her dressing-gown and stroked her knee. 'You have pretty knees. They're rare, pretty knees.'

'You have beautiful hands.'

He was not as well built as Jean-Charles—too thin; but his hands were delicate and strong, his face expressive, changing and sensitive, and his movements had a sinuous grace. He lived in a finely-differentiated world made up of half-shades and quarter-tones, delicate lights and shadows; whereas with Jean-Charles it was always high noon—a harsh, even glare.

'Would you like a drink?'

'No thanks; but you have one.'

He poured himself a bourbon on the rocks—a most unusual brand, it seemed. He took little interest in food, but he prided himself on knowing a great deal about wine and spirits. He sat down again at Laurence's feet.

'I'll bet you have never got drunk.'

'I don't care for drinking.'

'You don't care for it or you're afraid of it?'

She stroked his black hair—it was still childishly soft. 'Don't you play the psychologist with me.'

'The thing is you're not at all an easy little creature to understand. So young, so gay at times, so close; and then at others Minerva with her helmet on.'

At the beginning she had liked him to talk about her: all women like it, and Jean-Charles had by no means spoilt her in that respect; but really it was all very much beside the point. She knew only too well what Lucien was interested in, or rather what made him restless.

'Nonsense. It all depends on the way I've done my hair.'

He laid his head on her knees. 'Just for five minutes let me dream that we shall stay like this for the rest of our lives. Our hair will grow white without our even noticing it. You will be a delicious old lady.'

'Dream away, my pet.'

Why did he talk this nonsense? Love that had no end: it was like the song 'It doesn't exist, it doesn't exist.' But the longing voice aroused something in her mind—a confused echo as it were of something that she had known before, in another life, or perhaps that she was experiencing at this very moment on another planet. It was as all-pervasive and as noxious as a scent by night in a closed bedroom—the scent of hyacinths. She said rather sharply, 'You will get tired of me.'

'Never.'

'Don't be romantic.'

'The other day an old doctor poisoned himself, holding his wife's hand—she had died a week before. These things happen . . .'

'Yes, but what's the motivation?' she asked, laughing.

'I'm not joking,' he said, reproachfully.

She had allowed the conversation to take a foolishly sentimental turn and now it was not going to be easy to get away. 'I don't like thinking of the future: the present's enough for me,' she said, pressing her hand against Lucien's cheek.

'Really?' He gazed at her, and in his eyes her reflection shone with an almost unbearable brilliance. 'You aren't bored when you're with me?'

'What an extraordinary notion! There's no one I'm bored with less.'

'An odd reply.'

'Well, you ask odd questions. Did I seem to be bored

51

this evening?'

'No.'

It was fun talking with Lucien. Together they wondered about the people at Publinf and the firm's clients: they made up adventures for them. Or else Lucien told her about the novels he had read, or the places he had seen; and he knew how to pitch upon the detail that gave Laurence a fleeting wish to read or to travel. Just now he had been talking about Fitzgerald, whom she only knew by name; and she had been amazed that so improbable a life had in fact been lived.

'That was a lovely evening,' she said.

He started. 'Why do you say *was*? It's not over . . .'

'Two o'clock in the morning. Sweetheart, I have to go.'

'Do you mean you aren't going to stay and sleep here?'

'The children are too big: it's growing dangerous.'

'Oh, please do.'

'No.'

Often last year, when Jean-Charles was in Morocco, she used to say no. She would leave and then suddenly she would stop the car, turn round and run back up the stairs. He would clasp her in his arms. 'You've come back!' And she would stay until dawn. Because of the delight on his face. Today she would not come back. And he knew it.

'What? Aren't you going to spend any of these nights with me?'

She stiffened. He had convinced himself that while Jean-Charles was away she would spend the night with him. But she had promised nothing.

'Just think if my daughters had any idea . . . the danger's too great.'

'You didn't mind it last year.'

'I was bitterly sorry afterwards.'

They were both on their feet. He paced up and down the room and then stood in front of her, looking furious. 'Always the same story. A little adultery on the side, but fundamentally a good wife, a good mother. Why is there no word for a woman who's a bad lover, a bad mistress ...?' His voice died away: his eyes clouded. 'That means we shall never spend another night together. We shall never have a better opportunity.'

'Maybe we shall.'

'No, because you'll never see to it that we do. You don't love me any more: you might as well say it.'

'Then why am I here?'

'You don't love me as you used to. Ever since you came back from the holidays, nothing has been the same as it was before.'

'It certainly has. We had this squabble twenty times before the holidays. Let me put on my clothes.'

He poured himself out another glass while she went to the bathroom, with its shelves covered with bottles and pots. Lucien collected the lotions and creams that were given to Publinf by clients, partly for fun but also because he took scrupulous care of his person. Of course. I'd stifle my remorse if things were as they were before—the shattering emotion, the night on fire, whirlwinds and avalanches of longing and delight. For that kind of metamorphosis you can betray, lie, risk everything. But not for these merely pleasant caresses, not for a pleasure so very like that which she had with Jean-Charles. Not for these mild feelings that made up part of the ordinary daily round. 'Even adultery is functional,' she said to herself. These quarrels used to stir her terribly; now they were just irritating. By the time she returned to the bedroom he had finished his second glass.

'I understand, don't you worry. You wanted an affair because you were curious and because after all it's rather simple-minded never to have deceived your husband ... But nothing more. And like a poor half-wit there I was talking to you about eternal love.'

'It's not true.' She came close and kissed him. 'I'm very, very fond of you.'

'Very fond! I've never had anything but the crumbs of your life. I put up with that. But if you're going to give me even less, it would be better to break.'

'I do what I can.'

'You can't hurt your husband, nor your daughters: but as for making me suffer, that's fine.'

'I don't want you to suffer.'

'Oh really! You don't give a damn. I thought you were different from the others: at times it might almost have been said you had a heart. Nothing of the sort. A free, independent woman, making a success of life, what does she want to be bothered with a heart for?'

He talked on and on. When things went badly for Jean-Charles he shut up. Lucien talked. Two ways of coping. It's quite true that even when I was a child I learnt to control my heart. Was that a good thing or a bad? A pointless question: you can't remake yourself.

'You don't drink, you never fly off the handle, I've never seen you cry once: you're afraid of losing your grip on yourself: that's what I call refusing to live.'

This pierced her, though she could not quite say what part of her was affected. I can't help it. I am what I am.

He gripped her wrist. 'Don't you understand? I've been waiting for these nights all this last month. Every night I've dreamt of them.'

'All right, I was in the wrong. I ought to have warned you.'

'You didn't: so stay!'

She gently loosened his grip. 'You must see that if Jean-Charles grew suspicious, things would be impossible between you and me.'

'Since of course you would give me up?'

'Don't let's go over all that again.'

'No. I know very well that I've lost.' Lucien's face softened: there was nothing but profound sadness in his eyes now. 'I'll see you tomorrow, then,' he said.

'Tomorrow. We'll have a lovely evening.' She kissed him: he did not kiss her back, but looked at her sorrowfully.

She felt no pity, but rather, as she was going back to

her car, a kind of envy. She had suffered, that night at Le Havre, when he said he would rather break right away: it was at the very beginning of their affair; she was carrying out a survey into the sales of Mokeski coffee and he had gone with her. He wanted to break rather than depend on her husband and her children, rather than hang about and beg. 'I'm going to lose him!' She had felt a sharp stab as exact as a bodily wound. And then again last winter when she came back from Chamonix. That fortnight had been a torture, said Lucien; it was better to break off entirely. She had begged him not to; he had not given way; he had stayed ten days without speaking to her, ten days of hell. Nothing remotely like that noble anguish they set to music. It was rather on the squalid side—a dirty mouth, a tendency to be sick. But at least there was something to regret, something in the world that was worth its weight in sorrow. He is still feeling that fever, and despair, and hope. He is luckier than I.

'Why Jean-Charles rather than Lucien?' wondered Laurence, looking thoughtfully at her husband as he spread marmalade on a rusk. She was quite aware that in the end Lucien would break away from her and that he would love another woman. (Why me rather than someone else?) She acquiesced and indeed in the long run that was what she wanted. Only she wondered 'Why Jean-Charles?' The children had gone to Feuverolles the evening before with Marthe and the flat was very quiet. But the neighbours were making the most of Sunday to hammer on the party wall with all their might. Jean-Charles thumped the table. 'I've had enough of this! I'm going to beat them up!' He had been irritable ever since he came back; he snapped at the children, flew at Goya and went over his grievances again and again. Vergne was a genius, a man with great vision; but he was so uncompromising that in the end Dufrène was right—he never accomplished anything. The contractor had not accepted the whole of his plan quite unaltered: Vergne ought to have thought of his colleagues before abandoning the whole thing—it's a fortune that has slipped between our fingers.

'I'm going to try to get into Monnod's.'

'You used to say you were a terrific team and that the whole place was full of enthusiasm.'

'You can't live on enthusiasm. I'm worth more than I'm earning with Vergne. At Monnod's I should make at least twice as much.'

'We live very well as things are, you know.'

'We would live even better.'

Jean-Charles had made up his mind to leave Vergne, who had behaved so handsomely to him (what would have become of us when Catherine was born if it had not been for his advances?), but first he had to demolish him verbally. 'Everybody talks about these extraordinary ideas, and the papers are full of them—it's all very fine . . .'

Why Jean-Charles rather than Lucien? Sometimes the same chasm opened when she was with the one as when she was with the other, the same utter lack of communication; only between her and Jean-Charles there were the children, the future and their home—a powerful link; whereas with Lucien, once she no longer felt anything, she was in the company of a stranger. But what if it had been Lucien she had married? It would be neither better nor worse, she thought. Why one man rather than another? It was odd. You find yourself involved with a fellow for life just because he was the one you met when you were nineteen. She was not sorry that it had been Jean-Charles: far from it. So full of life and energy, his head crammed with plans and ideas, so wholly taken up with what he was doing, bright, popular with everyone he came into contact with. And faithful, straightforward, well built, an expert and frequent lover. He adored his home and his children and Laurence. Not in the same way as Lucien—less romantic but reliable and touching; he needed her presence and her approval; and as soon as he thought her sad or even withdrawn he became terribly worried. The ideal husband. She congratulated herself upon having married him, him and nobody else; but all the same she was amazed that something so important should depend upon mere chance. No particular reason about it. (But everything was like that.) These stories of twin souls—were they ever to be found outside books? Even the old doctor who had been killed by his wife's death: that did not prove they had been made for one another. 'To love with one's whole heart,' said Papa. Do I love Jean-Charles—did I love Lucien—with my whole heart? She had the feeling that people lived next to her, in juxtaposition, not in her heart, except for her daughters—but that must be physical.

'A man is not a great architect unless he can adapt himself.'

The ringing of the front-door bell interrupted Jean-Charles; he closed the sliding division that cut the room in two and Laurence brought Mona in to her study area.

'It's sweet of you to have come.'

'I wasn't going to leave you in the lurch.'

Mona was a charming little creature in these trousers and a massive pullover, tomboyish in outline, feminine in her smile and the graceful movement of her head. Usually she would not do the slightest thing outside office-hours—they exploit you enough without that. But the draft had to be delivered that evening at the latest and she knew that her dummy was not quite right. She looked round the room. 'Come, you do yourself proud.' After a moment's thought she added, 'Of course, with both of you earning, you must make quite a packet.'

No irony; no blame: she was making a comparison. She made quite a good living, but it appeared (she rarely spoke about herself) that she came from a very humble background and that she had an entire family on her hands. She sat down by Laurence and spread her drawings out on the desk. 'I've done several, with little variations.'

Launching a new brand of a product so common as tomato sauce was not an easy matter. Laurence had suggested that Mona should work on the sun/coolness contrast. The page she had produced was agreeable: in lively colours it showed a big sun in the sky, a high-perched village and olive-trees; in the foreground a tin with the brand-name and a tomato. But there was something lacking—the taste of the fruit, its juiciness. They had talked it over for a long while. And they had come to the conclusion that there had to be a cut in the skin of the tomato, so as to show some of its inside.

'Ah, that makes all the difference in the world!' said Laurence. 'You feel like biting it.'

'Yes, I thought you'd be pleased,' said Mona. 'Look at the others...' Each sheet had slight differences in colour and shape.

'It's hard to choose.'

Jean-Charles came in; as he warmly shook Mona's hand his teeth gleamed, shining white. 'Laurence has told me so much about you! And I've seen so many of your drawings. I adore your Méribel. You're very talented.'

'One bashes along,' said Mona.

'Which of these drawings would make you want to eat tomato sauce?' asked Laurence.

'They are all very much alike, aren't they? Very pretty, too: real little pictures.' Jean-Charles put his hand on Laurence's shoulder. 'I'm going down to clean the car. You'll be ready at half-past twelve? We mustn't start any later if we want to reach Feuverolles for lunch...'

'I'll be ready.'

He went out, beaming.

'Are you going to the country?' asked Mona.

'Yes. Mama has a house. We go almost every Sunday. It's a relaxation...' She was on the point of bringing out an automatic 'it's essential'. She heard Gilbert's voice, 'A relaxation that's essential.' She looked at Mona's tired face and she felt vaguely embarrassed. (No awkwardness there, no guilty conscience, no morose delectation.)

'It's terribly funny,' said Mona.

'What is?'

'It's terribly funny the way your husband is like Lucien.'

'You're wandering, my poor dear. Lucien and Jean-Charles, they're as different as chalk and cheese.'

'They're as like as two peas, as I see it.'

'I absolutely don't follow you at all.'

'They're both guys with pretty ways and white teeth; they know how to say the right thing and they both plaster themselves with that stuff after shaving.'

'Oh, if that's what you judge by ...'

'That's what I judge by.' She broke off. 'Well, which idea do you like best?'

Laurence looked through them again. So fine, so Lucien and Jean-Charles did both use after-shave. And Mona's boy-friend, what was he like? She wanted to make her talk, but now she had that reserved look that kept Laurence at a distance. What would she do with her Sunday?

'I think this is the best. Because of the village. I like the way the houses come tumbling down the slope ...'

'That's the one I like best, too,' said Mona. She gathered up her papers. 'Fine. I'm on my way.'

'Wouldn't you like a drink? Wine? Whisky? Or some tomato juice!' They laughed.

'No, I don't want anything really. But show me your nest.'

Mona walked from room to room, without saying anything. Sometimes she touched the stuff of a chair-cover or a curtain, or the wood of a table. In the sunlit drawing-room area she flopped into an easy chair. 'I can see why you don't understand anything at all.'

Generally speaking Mona was friendly, but there were moments when she seemed to detest Laurence. Laurence did not like being hated in general, and in particular she disliked being hated by Mona. Mona stood up, and as she buttoned her jacket she looked around with a final glance that Laurence could not make out: she was sure that at all events it was not one of envy.

Laurence took her as far as the lift and then went back to her desk. She put the maquette they had chosen and her copy into an envelope; she felt obscurely vexed. Mona's scornful voice: what gave her this notion of superiority? She was not a Communist; but all the same she must have some of that mystique of the proletariat, as Jean-Charles called it; there was something of the sectarian in her, and this was not the first time Laurence had noticed it. ('If there's anything I loathe, it's sectarianism,' said Papa.) A pity. That was what kept everyone imprisoned in his own little circle. Yet with a little good will on both sides it would be easy enough to get on, said Laurence to herself, sadly.

It's irritating, thought Laurence, but I never remember my dreams. Jean-Charles has one to tell every morning, a clearly defined dream, rather weird, like the ones you see on the cinema or read about. As for me—a blank. Everything that happens to me in the dark folds of the night, a blank: a real life to do with me that nevertheless slips through my fingers. If I knew about it maybe it would help me (to do what?). At all events she did know why she woke up in the morning with something hanging over her head: Dominique. Dominique, who had carved herself out a career with an axe, crushing everybody who stood in her way and trampling over them, and now all at once powerless, struggling furiously. She had seen Gilbert again 'as friends', and he had not told her the other woman's name. 'Does she even exist?' she asked me, suspiciously.

'Why should he lie to you?'

'He's so complicated.'

I asked Jean-Charles. 'Would you tell her the truth if you were in my place?'

'Certainly not. It's always best to be involved as little as possible in other people's business.'

Dominique was hanging on to a faint sort of hope, then. A very shaky one. On Sunday she had stayed shut in her room at Feuverolles, alleging a head-ache, shattered by Gilbert's absence and thinking 'He'll never come back.' On the telephone (she calls me every day) she describes him in such hideous terms that I find it difficult to see why she should want him at all: she says he is arrogant, full of admiration for himself, sadistic, madly selfish, and perfectly willing to sacrifice everybody for the sake of his own comfort and his whims. At other times she cries up his intelligence, his strength of mind and his brilliant success, and asserts, 'He will come back to me.' She is hesitating about what tactics to use, gentleness or violence. What will she do on the day—it won't be long now—when Gilbert tells her everything? Kill herself? Kill him? I can't visualize it at all. I've never known Dominique except on the top of the wave.

Laurence inspected the books Jean-Charles had recommended. (He had laughed. 'Ha, ha! So you have made up your mind? I'm so glad. You'll realize that after all we really are living in a pretty extraordinary age.' He looked little more than a boy when he was all enthusiastic like that.) She had leafed through them and she had looked at their conclusions: they said the same thing as Jean-Charles and Gilbert—everything was a great deal better than it had been before, and everything would be better still later on. Some countries had begun badly, particularly those of black Africa; the sudden abrupt rise in population in China and the whole of Asia was disturbing; but thanks to synthetic proteins, birth-control, automation, and atomic energy it was reasonable to think that by about 1990 the civilization of abundance and leisure would be in existence. The world would form a single entity, perhaps speaking (thanks to automatic translation) one universal language; men would have all they wanted to eat and they would only devote a trifling amount of their time to work; they would no longer suffer pain or illness. Catherine would still be young in

1990. Only it was today that she wanted to be comforted about what was going on around her. What I need is other books, to give me other points of view. What books? Proust can't help me. Nor Fitzgerald. Yesterday I stood there in front of the window of a big bookshop. *Masse et puissance: Bandoung: Pathologie de l'entreprise: Psychoanalyse de la femme: L'Amérique et les Américains: Pour une doctrine militaire française: Une nouvelle classe ouvrière: Une classe ouvrière nouvelle: L'Aventure de l'espace: Logique et structure: L'Iran ...* Which to start with? I did not go in.

Ask questions. But who to ask? Mona? She doesn't care for chat: she gets through the greatest amount of work in the shortest possible time. And I know what she would say. She would describe the state of the workers, which is not what it should be—a point upon which everybody agrees, although with the family allowances they almost all have a washing-machine, the television and even a car. Housing is inadequate, but the position is changing: you only have to look at the new blocks, the building-sites and the red-and-yellow cranes standing up against the Paris sky. Nowadays everybody is very much concerned with social questions. Fundamentally the only argument is as to whether or not everything is being done so that there should be more comfort and justice upon earth. Mona thinks not. Jean-Charles says, 'Society never does *everything* it can: but at present it is doing an enormous amount.' According to him people like Mona erred by being impatient: they were like Louise when she was astonished that men had not already landed on the moon. Yesterday he said to me, 'Of course, the human effects of high population density and automation are sometimes unfortunate, but who wants to hold up progress?'

Laurence took the latest issues of *L'Express* and *Candide* out of the rack. On the whole the papers—the dailies and the weeklies—agreed with Jean-Charles. Nowadays she opened them without dread. No, nothing dreadful was happening any more—except in Vietnam; but nobody in France approved of what the Americans were doing. She was glad that she had overcome that kind of fear which condemned her to ignorance (it was much more that than lack of time: you can always find time.) Basically all you had to do was to look at things objectively. The difficulty was that you could not get that across to a child. At present Catherine seemed calm. But if she were to get worried again I shouldn't be able to talk to her any better now than before...

Crisis between France and Algeria. Laurence had read half the article when there was a ring at the bell: two cheerful peals. Marthe. Laurence had asked her a dozen times not to come without warning. But she obeyed supernatural promptings; she had grown very peremptory since inspiration reached her from above.

'I'm not interrupting you?'

'A little. But since you're here stay five minutes.'

'Are you working?'

'Yes.'

'You work too much.' Marthe peered into her sister's face. 'Unless you have worries. You were not cheerful on Sunday.'

'Oh yes I was.'

'Come, come. Your little sister knows you very well.'

'You're mistaken.'

Laurence had no desire to confide in Marthe. And anyhow the words would instantly take on the wrong proportions—too big. If she were to say 'I'm anxious about Mama: Catherine worries me: Jean-Charles is horribly ill-tempered: I have a love-affair that is weighing on my mind,' it might be thought that her head was filled with a dense mass of preoccupations that took up her whole being. In fact the preoccupation was there without having a real presence—it was in the colour of the day and the air she breathed. She thought of it continually and she never thought of it at all.

'You know,' said Marthe, 'there is something I want to

talk to you about. I wanted to talk to you on Sunday, but you make me feel nervous.'

'I make you feel nervous?'

'Yes. Isn't it funny? And I know I'm going to make you cross. Well, never mind. Catherine will be eleven soon: I think you ought to send her to catechism-classes and let her take her first communion.'

'What an idea! Neither Jean-Charles nor I believe in religion.'

'But you had her christened for all that.'

'Because of Jean-Charles' mother. But now she's dead...'

'You are taking a grave responsibility on yourself by depriving your daughter of any religious instruction. We live in a Christian civilization. The majority of children take their first communion. Later on she will blame you for having decided for her, without leaving her the freedom of choice.'

'That's rich! So sending her to catechism-classes means leaving her free.'

'Yes. Because that's the normal attitude in France to-day. You're turning her into an exception, someone who's left out.'

'Don't go on so.'

'I'm going to go on. It seems to me that Catherine's sad and disturbed. She says some very curious things. I've never tried to influence her, but I listen. Death and evil are hard things for a child to face if there's no belief in God. If she did believe it would help her.'

'What curious things has she said?'

'I don't remember exactly.' Marthe looked closely at her sister. 'Haven't you noticed anything?'

'Of course I have. Catherine asks a great many questions. I will not answer them with lies.'

'You're rather arrogant, laying down that they are lies.'

'No more than you when you lay down that they are the truth.' Laurence touched her sister's arm. 'Don't let's argue. She's my daughter and I'm bringing her up as I think best. You can always fall back on praying for her.'

'And I don't fail to do so!'

What a nerve Marthe had! It was true that it was not easy to give children a secular upbringing in a world overrun by religion. Catherine was not tempted in that direction. As for Louise, she did find the picturesque side of the ceremonies alluring. At Christmas she would certainly ask to go to see the crèches ... From their earliest days Laurence had told them about the Bible and the Gospels at the same time as the classical myths and the life of Buddha. She had explained that they were beautiful legends that had grown up around real men and happenings. Her father had helped her in her explanations. And Jean-Charles had told them about the beginnings of the universe, from the nebulae to the stars and from matter to life: they had thought it a perfectly splendid story. Louise had grown particularly enthusiastic over a very simple astronomy book with lovely pictures. It was a long, combined, considered effort, one which Marthe had spared herself by entrusting her boys to priests and which she was ready to destroy with a flick of her fingers—unbelievably presumptuous.

'You really can't remember what Catherine said that particularly struck you?' asked Laurence a little later as she was going towards the door with her sister.

'No. It was more a kind of intuition I had, something beyond what was said,' replied Marthe, with a holy expression on her face.

Laurence shut the door, feeling irritated. When Catherine came back from school just now she seemed cheerful. She was waiting for Brigitte so they could do their Latin translation together. What would they talk about? What did they talk about? When Laurence questioned her Catherine was evasive. I don't think she distrusts me: it's rather that we lack a common language. I've let her run very free and at the same time I've treated her as a baby; I've not tried to talk to her: so I think words intimidate her, at least when I am there. I can't hit upon a point of contact—can't get through. *Crisis between France and Algeria*. Still, I should like to finish this article.

'*Bonjour m'dame*.' Brigitte held out a little bunch of Dresden daisies.

'Thank you: how sweet of you.'

'Look, I have sewn my hem.'

'Oh yes. It's really much better like that.'

When they had met in the entrance of the Musée de l'Homme the pin was still there in Brigitte's skirt. Laurence had not said anything, but the child had noticed her look and her ears had gone red.

'Oh, I've forgotten again . . .'

'Try and remember.'

'I promise I'll sew it up this evening.'

Laurence had shown them round the museum; Louise grew rather bored, the two others darted about, full of exclamations. That evening Brigitte said to Catherine, 'How lucky you are to have such a pet of a mother.'

One did not have to be a seer to detect the orphan child's uncertainty behind the grown-up ways.

'You're going to do a Latin translation?'

'Yes.'

'And then you'll gossip like a couple of old market-women.' Laurence hesitated. 'Brigitte, don't tell Catherine miserable things.'

Her whole face and even her neck flushed scarlet. 'What have I said that I oughtn't to have?'

'Nothing in particular.' Laurence smiled comfortingly. 'Only Catherine is still very young: she often cries at night: there are a great many things that frighten her.'

'Oh, I see.' Brigitte looked more disconcerted than sorry. 'But if she asks me questions am I to say you've told me not to answer?'

Now it was Laurence who was confused. I feel in the wrong for having put her in the wrong, whereas really . . . 'What questions?'

'I don't know. About what I've seen on the television.'

Oh yes, there was that too—the television. Jean-Charles often dreamt about what it might be, but he deplored what it actually was: he scarcely looked at anything but the news and one of the popular documentary programmes which Laurence watched too, occasionally. Sometimes they showed almost unbearable scenes: and for a child pictures were more striking than words.

'What have you seen on television these last few days?'

'Oh, lots of things.'

'Sad things?'

Brigitte looked straight at Laurence. 'I think lots of things are sad. Don't you?'

'Oh yes, of course I do.' What had they been showing recently? I ought to have watched. The famine in India? Massacres in Vietnam? Race-riots in the States? 'But I didn't watch the latest programmes,' she went on. 'What struck you particularly?'

'Those girls who put rounds of carrot on fillets of herring,' said Brigitte impulsively.

'How do you mean?'

'Just like that. They said how they put rounds of carrots on fillets of herring all day long. They were not much older than me. I'd rather die than live like that!'

'It can't be quite the same for them.'

'Why not?'

'They've been brought up differently.'

'They didn't look as though they liked it much,' said Brigitte.

Stupid occupations that would soon vanish with automation: meanwhile, of course ... The silence dragged on.

'All right. You go and do your translation. And thank you for the flowers,' said Laurence.

Brigitte did not move. 'I mustn't tell Catherine?'

'What about?'

'Those girls.'

'Of course you can,' said Laurence. 'It's only when there's something you think absolutely ghastly that it would be better to keep it to yourself. I'm afraid of Catherine having nightmares.'

Brigitte twisted her belt: usually she was very plain and direct, but now she seemed quite at a loss. 'I handled it badly,' thought Laurence. She was not pleased with herself; but how ought she to have set about it? 'Well, anyhow, I depend on you. Just take a little care, that's all,' she finished awkwardly.

Have I become insensitive, or is Brigitte unusually vulnerable, she asked herself when the door had closed again. 'Rounds of carrot all day long.' No doubt if girls earned their living like that it was because they were incapable of doing more interesting work. But that did not make it any the more amusing for them. This was another of those regrettable 'human effects'. Am I right or am I wrong to mind it so little?

Laurence read the rest of the article: once she had begun a thing she did not like to leave it unfinished. Then she set about her work—a script for a brand of shampoo. She smoked cigarette after cigarette: even foolish things become interesting if one tries to do them well. The packet was empty. It was late. There was a vague sort of noise coming from the far end of the flat. Was Brigitte still there? And what was Louise up to? Laurence crossed the hall. In her room Louise was weeping, and there were tears in Catherine's voice. 'Don't cry,' she was saying, 'I promise you I don't like Brigitte better than you.'

Well, there you are: but why do one person's pleasures always have to be paid for with the tears of others?

'Loulou, you're the one I love best. I like having Brigitte to talk to, but you're my own little sister.'

'Am I? Am I really?'

Laurence tiptoed away. The sweet sorrows of childhood, where kisses mingle with tears. It did not matter at all that Catherine was not working quite so well: her sensitivity was ripening; she was learning things that are not taught at school—learning to sympathize, comfort, give and take; catch the fleeting shades of meaning in voices and expressions. For a moment Laurence felt a warmth about her heart—a precious warmth, and so rare. What could she do so that later on Catherine would never be starved of it?

CHAPTER 3

Laurence was taking advantage of the children's absence
to tidy their rooms. Maybe Brigitte had not told Catherine about the television programme that had impressed
her so; in any case Catherine had not reacted much. She
had been in the highest spirits that morning as she and
Louise got into their grandfather's car: he was taking
them off for the week-end to see the châteaux of the
Loire. Laurence was the one who had let the story worry
her—rather foolishly, all things being considered. She
found it harder to bear the idea of a dull wretchedness
repeated day after day than that of great disasters, which
were after all the exception.

She wondered how other people coped with this kind
of wretchedness and she had questioned Lucien when she
was lunching with him on Monday. (Unpleasant, these
meetings. He's resentful, but he hangs on. Dominique,
ten years ago, 'Men, I'm fed to the teeth with them.' Get
there late, break appointments, give less and less: they
end up by getting sick of it. Personally I can't do it. One
of these days I shall have to make up my mind to the
downright break, using an axe.) He scarcely took any
interest at all in these questions, but still he did answer
me. A girl of sixteen condemned to an utterly stupid
blind-alley of a job—it was lousy, certainly; but basically
life was always lousy, and if it was not lousy for one
reason then it was for another. Take me: I have a little
money of my own and I earn plenty, and what good does
it do me since you don't love me? Who is happy? Do you
know any happy people? You yourself escape the full-
sized miseries by shutting your heart up tight: I don't
call that happiness. Your husband? Maybe: but if he
were to learn the truth it wouldn't please him all that

much. All lives are worth much the same, give or take a little. You said so yourself—it's pitiful to see people's motives, their wretched little fantasies, their illusions. They have nothing solid to grip on, nothing they really love: they wouldn't eat all these pills and tranquillizers if they were happy. There's the unhappiness of the poor. There's also the unhappiness of the rich. You ought to read Fitzgerald; he talks about it extraordinarily well. Yes, thought Laurence, there's some truth in what he says. Jean-Charles is often cheerful, but he's not really happy: too easily and violently put out by one thing or another for that. As for Mama, with her splendid flat, her clothes and her house in the country, imagine the hell that is waiting for her! And what about me? I don't know. I lack something that other people possess ... Unless ... Unless they don't have it either. Maybe when Gisèle Dufrène sighs 'It's wonderful,' and when Marthe stretches her big mouth into that luminous smile they are not really feeling any more than I do. Only Papa ...

Laurence had had him all to herself last Wednesday, once the children were in bed: Jean-Charles was dining out with some young architects. ('The vertical is out, the horizontal is out: architecture will be oblique or it will not exist at all.' He thought it rather absurd, but still, he said when he came home, they did have some interesting points of view.) Once again she tried to put his desultory replies into some sort of order. Whatever the country, capitalist or socialist, man was everywhere crushed by technology, made a stranger to his own work, imprisoned, forced into stupidity. The evil all arose from the fact that he had increased his needs rather than limiting them: instead of aiming at an abundance that did not and perhaps never would exist he should have confined himself to the essential minimum, as certain very poor communities still do. In Sardinia, for example, and in Greece— communities untouched by technology and uncorrupted by money. There the people did experience an austere happiness, because there certain values were maintained, the truly human values of dignity, brotherliness and generosity which gave life a unique savour. As long as fresh needs continued to be created, so new frustrations would come into being. When had the decline begun? The day knowledge was preferred to wisdom and mere usefulness to beauty. Along with the Renaissance, rationalism, capitalism and the worship of science. All right. But now things had reached that point, what was one to do? Try to revive wisdom and the love of beauty in oneself and in those around one. Only a moral revolution—not a social or a political or a technical revolution—only a moral revolution would lead man back to his lost truth. At least the individual could carry out this moral change on his own account: he would then accede to happiness, in spite of the surrounding world with all its absurdity and chaos.

Essentially what Lucien said and what Papa said coincided. Everyone was unhappy: everyone could find happiness—the one amounted to the other. Can I explain to Catherine that people are not so unhappy as all that since they cling to life? Laurence hesitated. It's the same as saying that unhappy people are not unhappy. Is that true? Dominique's voice all broken with sobs and cries: she loathed her life, but she had not the slightest wish to die: that is unhappiness. And again there is that emptiness, that void which freezes your heart and which is worse than death although you are preferring it to death so long as you do not kill yourself. I went through that five years ago and I still feel the horror of it. And the fact is that people do kill themselves—he asked for bananas and a towel—because in reality there does exist something worse than death. That is what chills your spine when you read an account of a suicide: not the frail corpse hanging from the window-bars but what happened inside that heart immediately before.

No, when I really think it over, said Laurence to herself, Papa's answers are only valid for himself: he has always borne everything stoically—his renal calculi and his operation, his four years in the Stalag and Mama's going, although that made him so sad. And it was only he who could take a vivid pleasure in that very austere, re-tired life that he had chosen for himself. I should like to know his secret. Perhaps if I were to see him more often, and for longer at a time ...

'Are you ready?' asked Jean-Charles. They went down to the garage: Jean-Charles opened the car door. 'Let me drive,' said Laurence. 'You're too much on edge.'

He smiled good-temperedly. 'As you like.' And he moved over. Having it out with Vergne must have been unpleasant: he did not talk about it, but he looked dark and gloomy and he drove dangerously fast, braking vio-lently and bursting into rages. The day before yesterday's papers might very easily have carried another account of a stand-up fight between drivers.

The other day, at Publinf, Lucien had given a brilliant explanation of the psychology of the man at the wheel—frustration, compensation, power and isolation. (He him-self was a very good driver, but absurdly fast.) Mona in-terrupted. 'I'll tell you why all these well-bred gentlemen turn into sods when they're behind a wheel.'

'Why?'

'Because they are sods.'

Lucien shrugged. What did she really mean?

'When I come back on Monday I sign up with Mon-nod,' said Jean-Charles cheerfully.

'Are you glad?'

'Oh, very. I'm going to spend Sunday sleeping and playing badminton. And on Monday I'll get off to a good start.'

The car came out of the tunnel: Laurence accelerated, scanning the driving-mirror. Overtake, fall back, over-take, overtake, fall back. Saturday evening: Paris was emptying. She loved driving and Jean-Charles did not possess that fault so common in husbands—whatever he thought he never uttered a word. She smiled. He did not have many faults, all in all; and when they were driving side by side she always had the illusion—though she was not much of a one for traps of this kind—that they were 'made for each other'. She thought firmly, 'This week I shall speak to Lucien.' Yesterday he had said, with blame in his voice, 'You don't love anyone!' Is that true? Not at all. I'm very fond of everybody. Except Gilbert.

She left the motorway and took a little deserted road. Gilbert would be at Feuverolles. Triumphantly Dominique had telephoned: 'Gilbert will be there.' Why was he coming? Maybe he was playing the friendship card: that wouldn't get him far the day the truth came out. Or was he in fact coming to tell her everything? Laurence's hands grew damp on the wheel. Dominique had only been able to hang on this last month because she still had some hope.

'I wonder why Gilbert agreed to come.'

'Perhaps he's given up his plans for marriage.'

'I doubt that.'

It was cold and dreary; the flowers were dead; but the windows gleamed in the darkness and a huge fire of logs blazed in the living-room. Not many people, but those of the best—the Dufrènes, Gilbert, Thirion and his wife: Laurence had known him when she was a child. He had been one of her father's colleagues; and now he was the best-known barrister in France. Marthe and Hubert had not been asked this time. They were not up to the mark. Smiles, greetings: Gilbert kissed the hand Laurence had refused him a month ago. His look was full of meaning when he said, 'Would you like something to drink?'

'Presently,' said Dominique. She seized Laurence's shoulder. 'Come upstairs first and do your hair—it's all untidy.' In the bedroom she smiled. 'Your hair is perfectly all right. I wanted to talk to you.'

'What's wrong?'

'What a pessimist you are!' Dominique's eyes were shining. She was a little over-dressed in her 1900 blouse and her long skirt (who was she copying?). In an excited voice she said, 'Just imagine! I've discovered the secret.'

74

'Really?' How could Dominique possibly have this roguish look on her face if she knew everything?'

'You'll be amazed, absolutely amazed.' She paused deliberately. 'Gilbert has gone back to his old flame. It's Lucile de Saint-Chamont.'

'What's made you think that?'

'Oh, I've been told. He's at her place all the time. He spends his week-ends at the Manoir. Amusing, isn't it? After everything he's told me about her! I wonder how she set about it. She's cleverer than I thought.'

Laurence was silent. She loathed the unfair superiority of the one who knows over the one who does not. Open her eyes? Not today, with all those guests in the house.

'Perhaps it's not Lucile but one of her friends.'

'Oh come! She would never encourage an affair between Gilbert and another woman. I can see why he hid her name: he was afraid I should laugh in his face. I can hardly understand this weird business at all; but at all events it can't last. If Gilbert dropped her as soon as he got to know me, that was because he had his reasons, and they're still valid. He'll come back to me.'

Laurence said nothing. The silence dragged on. Dominique ought to have been surprised by it, but no, not at all: she was so used to asking the questions and giving the replies ... In a musing voice she went on, 'It might be worth while sending Lucile a letter describing her anatomy and her tastes in detail.'

Laurence gave a start. 'You'd never do that!'

'It would be fun. Just imagine Lucile's face! Imagine Gilbert's! No. He'd never forgive me. My tactics will be quite the reverse: I'll be very sweet. Regain lost ground. I have great hopes of the trip to the Lebanon.'

'You think it'll come off?'

'What? Of course!' Dominique's voice rose. 'He's promised me this Christmas at Baalbek for months and months. Everybody knows about it. He can't cry off now.'

'But she'll be against it.'

'I'll force him to choose: either he goes to the Lebanon

'with me or I don't see him any more.'

'He won't give in to blackmail.'

'He doesn't want to lose me. This thing with Lucile isn't serious.'

'Then why did he tell you about it?'

'Out of sadism, to some extent. And then he needed free time, particularly his week-ends. But as you see I only had to press him a little and he came.'

'Well then, force him to choose,' said Laurence.

Maybe that was a solution. Dominique would have the satisfaction of thinking that she was the one who did the breaking off. Later, when she learnt the truth, the worst would be over.

The living-room was full of laughter and the sound of voices: they were drinking wine, bourbon, martinis: Jean-Charles passed Laurence a glass of pineapple-juice. 'Nothing unpleasant?'

'No. Nothing pleasant, either. Look at her.'

Dominique had put her hand on Gilbert's arm with a possessive gesture. 'When I think you haven't been here for three weeks! You work too hard. You must learn how to relax as well.'

'I know. I know,' he said in a flat, expressionless voice.

'No you don't. The country is the only thing that really sets you up.' She smiled at him with a rather arch coquetry quite new to her. It did not suit her in the least. She was talking very loudly. 'Or travelling,' she added. Still holding on to Gilbert's arm she said to Thirion, 'We are going to spend Christmas in the Lebanon.'

'A wonderful idea. They say it's splendid.'

'Yes. And I particularly want to see Christmas in a hot country. One always imagines Christmas with snow about . . .'

Gilbert made no reply. Dominique was so tense that a single word might send her off. He must be aware of it.

'Our friend Luzarches has had a marvellous idea,' said the blonde Mme Thirion in her singsong voice. 'A surprise Christmas by plane. He's taking twenty-five of us aboard, and we don't know whether we shall come down at London, Rome, Amsterdam or where. And of course he will have taken tables in the best restaurant in the town.'

'Fun,' said Dominique.

'Generally speaking people have so little imagination when it comes to having fun,' said Gilbert.

Here was still another of those words whose meaning Laurence did not grasp. Sometimes a film was interesting or it made you laugh; but as for having fun ... Did Gilbert have fun? Getting into a plane without knowing where it was going, was that fun? The suspicion that had come into her mind the other day ... perhaps it was well-based.

She went and sat with Jean-Charles and the Dufrènes by the fire.

'What a pity that one can't treat oneself to an open fire in modern buildings,' said Jean-Charles. He gazed into the flames, and the firelight danced on his face. He had taken off his suède jacket and undone the collar of his American shirt; he looked younger and more at his ease than usual. (The same applied to Dufrène, who was wearing corduroy: was it simply a question of their clothes?)

'I've forgotten to tell you a story your father will love,' said Jean-Charles. 'Goldwater is so fond of wood fires that in summer he freezes his house with the air-conditioning and lights huge blazes everywhere.'

Laurence laughed. 'Yes, Papa will like that...'

On a low table by her side there were magazines—*Réalité*, *L'Express*, *Candide*, *Votre Jardin*—and a few books, the Goncourt and the Renaudot, the well-known prize-winners of the year. Records were scattered over the divan, although Dominique never listened to music. Laurence looked in her direction again: she was smiling, talking away, very self-possessed, gesticulating a great deal. 'Well, for my part I'd rather dine at Maxim's. At least I'm sure the chef hasn't spat into the food, and my knees aren't rubbing against those of the man at the next table. I know that there's a silly fashion for little bistrots at the moment; but they're just as expensive, they smell of burnt fat, and you can't move an inch without banging into someone else.'

'You don't know Chez Gertrude?'

'Of course I do. But at that price I'd rather have La Tour d'Argent.'

She seemed wholly at ease. Why had Gilbert come? Laurence heard Jean-Charles and the Dufrènes laughing. 'No, but seriously,' said Jean-Charles, 'do you realize what things are coming to? What with the contractors, the promoters, the managers and the engineers, where do we poor architects come in?'

'Oh, those promoters!' sighed Dufrène.

Jean-Charles poked the fire: his eyes were shining. Were there wood fires in his childhood? In any case there was a look of childhood on his face, and Laurence felt something melt within her: tenderness. If only she had found it again, and this time for ever ... Dominique's voice jerked her out of her daydream.

'I didn't think it would be any sort of fun either, and it began badly, with the arrangements nearly breaking down so that we stood about for an hour before we went in. Still, it was worth going—everybody who counts in Paris was there. The champagne was respectable. And I must say I thought Mme de Gaulle much better than I had expected: no style, of course—she's not Linette Verdelet—but she does have masses of dignity.'

'They tell me that only finance and politics were allowed anything to eat: the arts and letters were merely given drinks—is that right?' asked Gilbert carelessly.

'Nobody went there just to eat,' said Dominique with a curt, nervous laugh.

What a swine that Gilbert was: he had asked Mama that question merely to be unpleasant! Dufrène turned towards him. Is it true that they're thinking of using IBM machines to paint abstract pictures?'

'It could be done. Only I don't imagine it would pay,'

said Gilbert, with a complacent smile.

'What! A machine can paint!' cried Mme Thirion.

'Abstract paintings. Why not?' said Thirion with an ironic smile.

'Did you know that there are some that turn out Mozart and Bach?' said Dufrène. 'There are indeed: the only trouble is that their productions are faultless, whereas flesh and blood composers make errors all the time.'

Why, I read that not long ago in a weekly. Since she had taken to looking at the papers again Laurence had observed that people often reproduced the articles in their talk. Well, why not? They had to get their information from somewhere.

'Presently machines will take over from our studios and we'll be out of a job,' said Jean-Charles.

'That's quite certain,' said Gilbert. 'We are on the threshold of a new epoch—one in which men will become useless.'

'Not us!' said Thirion. 'There will always be lawyers, because a machine will never be capable of eloquence.'

'But maybe people will no longer be sensitive to eloquence,' said Jean-Charles.

'Oh, come! Man is a talking animal and he will always let himself be swayed by the power of the word. Machines won't change human nature.'

'That's just what they will do!'

Jean-Charles and Dufrène were in agreement (they read the same periodicals): the idea of what constituted man was due to be overhauled and no doubt it would vanish; it was a nineteenth-century invention and now it was out of date. In every field—writing, music, painting, architecture—art was rejecting the humanism of the earlier generations. Looking indulgent, Gilbert remained silent: eagerly the others interrupted one another. You must admit that there are books that can no longer be written, films no one can look at any more, music that no one can listen to: but masterpieces never date: what is a masterpiece? Subjective criteria ought to be done away with, that's impossible, I can't agree—the whole of modern criticism aims at exactly that, and what about the criteria for the Goncourt and the Renaudot—I'd like to know what they are, the prizes are even worse than last year, oh the whole thing is a put-up job on the part of the publishers, you know, I have it on absolutely sound authority that some members of the jury are bribed, its shameful, with painters it's even more scandalous, publicity can make a genius of any dauber whatever, if everybody takes him for a genius he *is* a genius, what a paradox; not at all, there's no other criterion, no objective criterion.

'Oh, come! Really: What is beautiful is beautiful!' cried Mme Thirion with such fervour that for a moment everybody was silent. Then the run of talk flowed on . . .

As usual Laurence's thoughts grew muddled: she was almost always against the person who was speaking, but as they did not agree among themselves she, by contradicting them, ended up by contradicting herself. Although Mme Thirion is a notorious fool I am tempted to say with her *what is beautiful is beautiful*. What is true is true. But what's the value of that opinion? Where do I get it from? From Papa; from school; from Mlle Houchet. I had convictions when I was eighteen. There was something of them left to her: not much—more a longing memory. She had no confidence in her judgments: it was so much a question of mood and circumstance. When I come out of a cinema I can hardly say whether I liked the film or not.

'Can I speak to you for a couple of minutes?'

Laurence stared coldly at Gilbert. 'I haven't the least wish to talk.'

'I insist.'

Out of curiosity and out of anxiety Laurence followed him into the next room. They sat down: she waited.

'I wanted to warn you that I'm going to break it to Dominique. There's no question of this trip, of course. And then Patricia is a very understanding, warm person, but she feels she's waited long enough. We want to get married at the end of May.'

Gilbert's decision was irrevocable. The only cure would be to kill him: Dominique would suffer much less. 'Why did you come?' she murmured. 'You are giving her false hopes.'

'I've come because for a variety of reasons I don't choose to make an enemy of Dominique: and she has brought our friendship into this. If I can manage this break gently, thanks to a few concessions, it would be much better, particularly for her, don't you think?'

'You can't do it.'

'Yes, I think I can,' he went on in another tone. 'I also came here to find out about her state of mind. She persists in believing that this is an ordinary little affair. I must open her eyes.'

'Not now!'

'I'm going back to Paris this evening...' Gilbert's face lit up. 'I tell you what, I am just wondering whether in Dominique's interest it would not be as well for you to prepare her.'

'Oh, so that's why you're really here: you want to get me to do your dirty work.'

'I must admit I hate scenes.'

'Because you have no imagination: the scenes aren't the worst part at all.' Laurence thought for a moment. 'Do just one thing: say no to the journey without telling her about Patricia. Dominique will be so angry that she'll break of her own accord.'

'You know very well that's not so,' said Gilbert sharply.

He was right. For a moment Laurence had wanted to believe in Dominique's 'I'll make him choose'; but she knew that after scenes and rows Dominique would in fact go on being patient, demanding, and hopeful.

'It's atrocious, what you're going to do.'

'I find your enmity very hurting,' said Gilbert, with a wounded look. 'No one can command his affections. I don't love Dominique any more: I do love Patricia.

Where's my crime?' There was something obscene about the word love in his mouth. Laurence stood up. 'I shall talk to her in the coming week,' said Gilbert. 'And I strongly advise you to go and see her as soon as we've had it out.'

Laurence gave him a look of hatred. 'So as to prevent her killing herself and leaving a note to say why? It would look bad, blood on Patricia's white dress...' She left the room. There were crayfish creaking in her ears, a hideous sound of inhuman suffering. She went to the buffet and poured herself a glass of champagne. They were filling their plates as they carried on with a conversation that had already begun.

'The child's not without talent,' said Mme Thirion, 'but she ought to be taught how to dress: she's capable of wearing a spotted blouse with a striped skirt.'

'It can be done, you know,' said Gisèle Dufrène.

'If you are an absolutely brilliant dressmaker you can do anything,' said Dominique. She came up to Laurence. 'What did Gilbert say to you?'

'Oh, he asked me to do something for a friend's niece who wants to get into publicity.'

'Really?'

'You don't suppose Gilbert would tell me about his relations with you?'

'Anything's possible with him. Aren't you eating anything?'

Laurence's appetite had been taken away. She dropped into an armchair and picked up a magazine. She felt that she could not possibly carry on a conversation. He was going to tell her during the week. Who could help me calm Dominique? During this last month Laurence had come to realize how lonely her mother was. Innumerable contacts: not a single friend. No one who could listen to her or even take her mind off her sorrow. One's life: what a frail, threatened construction to carry all alone. Was it like that for everyone? At least I do have Papa. And besides Jean-Charles would never make me unhappy. She looked up at him. He was talking, he was laughing and the people around him were laughing: as soon as he chooses to take the trouble, people like him. Once again her heart flooded with tenderness. After all it was natural enough that he should have been edgy these last few days. He knew what he owed Vergne; but still he could not sacrifice all his ambitions for Vergne's sake. It was this conflict that had upset him. He liked success and that was something Laurence sympathized with. Work would be terribly boring if one did not play the game all out, passionately.

'My dear Dominique,' said Gilbert ceremoniously, 'I am very sorry, but I simply must go.'

'Already?'

'I came early because I had to leave in good time to get back to Paris,' said Gilbert. He made brisk farewells all round. Dominique went out of the house with him. Jean-Charles beckoned Laurence. 'Come over here. Thirion is telling us fascinating anecdotes about his cases.'

They were all sitting down except Thirion, who paced to and fro, fluttering the sleeves of an imaginary robe. 'What do I think of my woman collegues, my dear lady?' he said to Gisèle. 'I have the highest opinion of them: many are quite charming and many are talented (generally speaking they are not the same ones). But one thing is certain: there is not one of them who will ever be able to argue a case before the assizes. They have not the necessary weight, nor authority, nor—and this will surprise you—the necessary theatrical feeling.'

'Women have succeeded in professions that seem on the face of it impossible for them,' said Jean-Charles.

'You can take the cleverest, the most silver-tongued of the lot, and I promise you that in front of a jury I'd destroy her in under two minutes.'

'Perhaps there are surprises waiting for you,' said Jean-Charles.

'Personally, I believe the future belongs to women.'

'Maybe. But only on condition that they don't ape the

men,' said Thirion.

'Having a man's profession isn't aping men.'

'Come, Jean Charles,' said Gisèle Dufrène, 'don't tell me you're a feminist, you who are so very up-to-date. Feminism is terribly old hat nowadays.'

Feminism: at present everybody was talking about it all the time. Laurence at once detached herself from the conversation. It was like psychoanalysis, the Common Market and the French atomic bomb: she did not know what to think; her mind was blank. I'm allergic. She looked at her mother, who was coming back into the room, a strained smile on her face. Tomorrow, the day after, this week anyhow, Gilbert is going to tell her everything. Her voice had rung out there in the silence/rest area, and it would ring out again: the swine! the swine! In her mind's eye Laurence saw the flowers that looked like evil birds. When she came back to the present, Mme Thirion was holding forth vehemently. 'I think this systematic running-down is utterly disgusting. After all, it's a charming idea: at the Hungry Childhood dinner on January 25 they are going to give us the little Indians' menu for our twenty thousand francs—a bowl of rice and a glass of water. Well, the left-wing press is sniggering about it. What would they say if we ate caviar and foie gras?'

'Everything can always be criticized,' said Dominique. 'The only thing to do is take no notice.' Her thoughts seemed far away, and as the others settled down to bridge she answered Mme Thirion more or less at random. Laurence opened *L'Express*: the news, dealt out in slim lines, could be swallowed like a glass of milk—no roughness, nothing that stuck, nothing that rasped. She was sleepy and she stood up eagerly when Thirion rose from the bridge-table saying, 'I have a heavy day tomorrow. We shall have to be getting along.'

'I'm going to bed,' she said.

'You must sleep wonderfully here,' said Mme Thirion. 'I imagine there's no need for sleeping-pills. In Paris it's impossible to do without them.'

'Personally I've cut them out ever since I took to having a harmonizer every day,' said Gisèle Dufrène.

'I tried one of those lullaby records, but it didn't lull me at all,' said Jean-Charles cheerfully.

'I've heard of an astonishing machine,' said Thirion. 'You plug it in and it produces fascinating, monotonous light-signals that send you to sleep; and it switches itself off automatically. I'm going to order one.'

'Oh, I shan't need anything of that kind tonight,' said Laurence. Delightful, these bedrooms: *toile de Jouy* on the walls, rustic beds with patchwork counterpanes, a china basin and ewer on the washstand. An almost invisible door in the wall led to the bathroom. She leant out of the window and breathed in the cold smell of earth. Jean-Charles would be there in a moment: she only wanted to think of him now, and his sideways face lit up by the dancing gleam of the fire. And suddenly there he was: he took her in his arms, and the tenderness became a molten flood coursing through Laurence's veins: and as their lips came together she staggered with desire.

'Well, there you are, my poor child! You weren't too frightened?'

'No,' said Laurence. 'I was so glad I hadn't run over the cyclist.' She leant her head against the back of the comfortable leather armchair. She was no longer quite so glad, though she could hardly tell why.

'Would you like a cup of tea?'

'Oh, don't bother.'

'It will only take five minutes.'

Badminton, television: it was already dark when we left; I was not driving fast. I could feel the presence of Jean-Charles there beside me, and I was thinking of our night while at the same time my eyes scanned the road in front. Suddenly a red-headed cyclist shot into the beam of my headlights from a track on the right. I gave the wheel

a violent turn, the car shot across the road and overturned in the ditch.

'Are you all right?'

'Fine,' said Jean-Charles. 'What about you?'

'Fine.'

He switched off the ignition. The door opened. 'Are
you hurt?'

'No.'

A party of cyclists, youths and girls, were standing
round the car as it lay there motionless, upside-down,
with its wheels still turning: 'You utter fool!' I shouted
at the red-haired boy, but what a relief! I had really
believed that I had run him over. I flung myself into Jean-
Charles' arms. 'Such luck, darling. Not a scratch!'

He did not smile. 'The car's wrecked.'

'Oh, the car—yes. But that's better than if it were you
or me.'

Some motorists had stopped: one of the youths explained. 'This fool here wasn't looking where he was
going. He shot in front of the car, so the young lady went
over to the left.'

The red-head stammered out apologies; the others
thanked me ... 'He owes you his life!'

At the side of that wet road, next to the shattered car, I
felt happiness bubbling up inside me, as intoxicating as
champagne. I loved the idiot cyclist because I had not
killed him, and his friends, who were smiling at me, and
these unknown people who were offering to take us back
to Paris. And suddenly my head swam and I lost con-
sciousness.

She had come to again in the back of a DS. But she
could not remember the journey back very clearly: after
all she had suffered a shock. Jean-Charles said they would
have to buy another car and that they would not get two
hundred thousand francs for the wreck; he was vexed,
understandably; but what Laurence found less accept-
able was that he seemed to be cross with her. After all, it
was not my fault; indeed I'm rather proud of having

landed us in the ditch so gently: but when all is said and done every husband is convinced that he can handle a car better than his wife. Yes, now I come to think of it he was so morally dishonest that when I observed, just before we went to bed, 'Nobody could have got out of that one without smashing the car,' he replied, 'It really doesn't seem very clever to me. We only have a third-party-collision policy.'

'You wouldn't really have wanted me to kill the boy?'

'You wouldn't have killed him. You might have broken his leg...'

'I might perfectly well have killed him.'

'Well, it would have served him right. Everybody would have given evidence in your favour.'

He said that without really believing a word of it, merely to be beastly to me, because he is convinced I could have got out of it with less damage. And that is untrue.

'Here's the tea—special mixture,' said her father, putting the tray down on a table littered with papers. 'You know what I wonder?' he said. 'If you had had the children in the car, would you have reacted in the same way?'

'I don't know,' said Laurence. She paused. Jean-Charles is a part of me, another self, she thought. We make a whole. I behaved as if I had been alone. But to put my daughters in danger to spare someone I'd never even seen —how absurd! But what about Jean-Charles? He was the one who was sitting in the suicide seat. He has something to be cross about, after all.

Her father went on, 'Yesterday, with the children, I would have mown down a whole orphanage rather than take the slightest risk.'

'How delighted they were!' said Laurence. 'You treated them like queens.'

'Oh, I took them to one of those little inns where you still eat real cream, and chickens fed on good corn, and real eggs. Do you know that in the States they feed chickens on seaweed and that the eggs have to be injected with a chemical to make them taste of egg?'

'That doesn't surprise me. When she came back from New York Dominique brought me chocolate chemically flavoured with chocolate.'

They laughed together. And to think that I've never spent a week-end with him! He poured the tea into cups that didn't match. A bulb set in an old oil lamp lit the table with an open volume of the Pléiade collection—he had the whole set. No need for him to rack his imagination to have fun.

'Louise is an uncommonly knowing little creature,' he said. 'But it's Catherine who is most like you. When you were that age you had the same gravity.'

'Yes, I was like her,' said Laurence. (Will she be like me?)

'It seems to me that her imagination has developed a great deal.'

'Do you know what? Marthe is begging and praying me to let her take her first communion.'

'She dreams of converting us all. She doesn't preach: she offers herself as an example. As who should say "Look how faith transfigures a woman and observe the degree of inner beauty she attains." But it's not easy to make inner beauty outwardly apparent, poor thing.'

'How unkind you are!'

'Oh, she's a good girl. Your mother and you have brilliant careers: being the mother of a family is rather dreary. So she stakes everything on holiness.'

'And having Hubert as the one and only witness of her life is obviously not enough.'

'Who was there at Feuverolles?'

'Gilbert Mortier, the Dufrènes, Thirion and his wife.'

'She invites that low scoundrel to her place? You remember when he used to come to the house—always prating, and never anything behind it. Without boasting I can say I had a better beginning than Thirion. His whole career has been made up of dirty jobs and schemes and publicity. And that's what Dominique wanted me to become!'

'You couldn't have.'

'I could if I had swum about in the same muck as Thirion.'

'That's what I mean.'

Dominique's utter want of understanding. 'He's chosen mediocrity.' No. A life with no dirty compromises, a life with time to think, with time for cultivated leisure, instead of that hectic existence they lead in Mama's set; and that I lead too.

'Is your mother flourishing?'

Laurence hesitated. 'Things are not going well with her and Gilbert Mortier. I think he's going to leave her.'

'She must be struck all of a heap! She's brighter than Miss World and pleasanter to look at than the late Mrs. Roosevelt, so she thinks herself better than any woman on earth.'

'For the moment she's very unhappy.' Laurence understood her father's hardness; but Dominique was a pitiful sight. 'You know, I have been thinking of what you said to me about unhappiness. It does exist, all the same. As for you, you can cope with anything—dominate any situation, but that's not within everybody's reach.'

'What I can do anyone can do. I'm not exceptional.'

'I think you are,' said Laurence affectionately. 'Take solitude, for example: there are not many people who can put up with it.'

'Because they don't really try wholeheartedly. My greatest happinesses have come to me when I have been alone.'

'Are you really contented with your life?'

'I've never done anything that I reproach myself for.'

'You're lucky.'

'You're not content with yours?'

'Oh, but I am! Only I do reproach myself for things—I don't look after my children as well as I ought; I neglect you.'

89

'You have your home and your job.'

'Yes; but still . . .'

Without Lucien I should have more time to myself, she reflected; I should see more of Papa, and I could read and think, as he does. My life is too cluttered up.

'For example, I have to go back this very minute,' she said, getting to her feet. 'Your special mixture was delicious.'

'But tell me, are you sure there's no internal damage? You ought to go and see a doctor.'

'No, no. I'm perfectly all right.'

'What are you going to do without a car? Would you like me to lend you mine?'

'I shouldn't like to deprive you of it.'

'No deprivation at all—I use it so rarely. I so much prefer strolling along the streets.'

That's quite typical of him, she thought affectionately as she settled behind the wheel. He's not taken in by anyone, and indeed he can be rough on occasion; but so alert, so attentive and always so ready to be kind. She still felt the warm twilight of the flat around her. Unclutter my life. I must get rid of Lucien.

'This very evening,' she had decided. She had said she was going out with Mona: Jean-Charles believed her—he always believed her, out of lack of imagination. He quite certainly did not deceive her, and the idea of being jealous never entered his mind for a moment.

'Quite an attractive place, don't you think?'

'Very attractive,' she said.

After they had spent an hour at Lucien's flat she had insisted upon going out. It seemed to her that it would be easier to say what she had to say in a public place rather than in the intimacy of a bedroom. He had taken her to a rather grand nightclub decorated in the 1900 manner, with subdued lights, mirrors, greenery and discreet recesses with sofas. She might have thought it up as the background for a film boosting a brand of champagne or old brandy. That was one of the snags of her job: she knew too much about how a set was put together—it fell to pieces under her eyes.

'What will you drink? They have some remarkable whiskies.'

'Order me one: you can drink it.'

'You're particularly lovely this evening.'

She smiled pleasantly. 'You tell me that every time.'

'It's true every time.'

She glanced at herself in the mirror. *A pretty, discreetly gay young woman, rather temperamental and rather mysterious: that's how Lucien sees me. I used to like that. For Jean-Charles she was efficient, straight, as open as the day. That was false, too. Pleasant to look at, yes. But plenty of women were better looking.* A dark girl with a pearly sheen and immense green eyes framed in huge false lashes was dancing with a boy a little younger than herself: *I can understand a man losing his head over someone like that. They were smiling at one another and sometimes their cheeks touched. Was that love? We are smiling at one another too, our hands touch.*

'If only you knew what a torment they are, these week-ends! Saturday night ... other nights I can remain in doubt about. But on Saturdays I'm certain. It's a red, flaming pit at the end of my week. I got drunk.'

'You were quite wrong to do so. It really doesn't matter all that much.'

'I don't suppose it really matters all that much with me, either.'

She did not reply. *What a bore he was becoming! Perpetual reproaches. If he utters another I'll go right on and say 'You're right...'*

'Come and dance?' he said.

'All right.'

This very evening, she repeated to herself. *Why, exactly? Not because of the night at Feuverolles: it did not bother her at all, going from one bed to another—it was so very much the same thing. And Jean-Charles had* chilled her to the heart after the accident, when she threw herself into his arms and he said coldly 'The car's wrecked.' The real reason, the only reason, was that love was an appalling bore once you had ceased loving. All that time wasted. They were silent, as they had so often been silent together; but was he aware that this was not the same silence?

And now how should I set about it? she wondered as she sat on the sofa again. She lit a cigarette. In old-fashioned novels people were always lighting cigarettes: it's a mere convention said Jean-Charles. But you do it often in real life when you need to keep yourself in countenance.

'You use a Criquet too?' said Lucien. 'You with such good taste? They're so ugly.'

'It's handy.'

'I should so love to give you a beautiful lighter. A really beautiful one. Gold. But I'm not even allowed to give you a present.'

'Oh, come, come! You haven't done badly.'

'Only nonsense.'

Scent, scarves: she said they were advertising samples. But obviously Jean-Charles would have been startled by a golden powder-case or cigarette-lighter.

'I don't feel strongly about things, you know. Advertising them has sickened me...'

'I don't really see the connection. Take a beautiful object—it lasts, it's crammed with memories. This lighter, for example: I lit your cigarette with it the first time you came to my place.'

'One doesn't need that to remember.'

Fundamentally Lucien lives outside himself, though his way of doing it is not the same as Jean-Charles'. Papa is the only person I know who is different. His loyalties are in himself, not in things.

'Why are you talking to me like this?' asked Lucien. 'You wanted to go out: we have gone out: I'm doing everything you want. You might be a little more agreeable.' She made no reply. 'All this evening you haven't said a single affectionate word.'

'There hasn't been an occasion.'

'There never will be an occasion any more.'

Now's the time, she said to herself. He'll suffer a little and then he'll get over it. At this very moment there are masses of lovers in the act of breaking off: in a year's time it will have vanished from their minds.

'I tell you what, you never stop reproaching me. It would be better for us to have things out frankly.'

'I've got nothing to have out,' he said hotly. 'And I'm not asking you anything.'

'Yes you are, indirectly. And I want to answer. I have the greatest affection for you and I always will have; but I'm not in love with you any more.' (Was I ever? Have those words any meaning?)

There was a silence. Laurence's heart beat a little faster, but the worst was over. The final words had been said. All that remained was to wind up the scene, end it, settle it for good.

'I've known that for a long while. Why do you feel you have to tell me so this evening?'

'Because we have to take things to their logical conclusion. If it's no longer a question of love, then it's better not to go to bed together any more.'

'But I do love you. And there are plenty of people who go to bed together without being madly enamoured.'

'I can't see any reason for doing so.'

'Of course! You've got all you need at home. And I—I who can't do without you any more—I'm the very least of your worries.'

'Not at all: it's primarily of you that I'm thinking. I give you much too little crumbs, as you often say yourself. Another woman would make you much happier.'

'What moving tenderness!' Lucien's face fell to pieces: he took Laurence's hand. 'You're not speaking seriously! Our whole relationship, those nights at Le Havre, the nights at my place, our adventure in Bordeaux—you're wiping all that out?'

'Oh, no. I shall always remember it.'

'You've forgotten already.'

He was bringing forward the past, he was struggling: she played her part calmly. It was perfectly useless, but she knew what was due to the person you leave; she would listen to him politely until the end—that was the least she could do. He looked at her suspiciously. 'I see! There's another man!'

'Oh dear, oh dear! With the life I lead?'

'No: no. I suppose not. You did not love me. You do not love anyone. There are some women who are frigid in bed. With you it's worse. You suffer from frigidity in the heart.'

'That's not my fault.'

'And what if I told you I was going to smash myself up on the motorway?'

'You wouldn't be as stupid as that. Come, don't make a terrific thing of it. One woman lost ... People are so very interchangeable, you know.'

'That's appalling, what you've just said.' Lucien stood up. 'Let's go. You'll make me want to hit you.'

They drove to Laurence's house in silence. She got out and hesitated for a moment on the edge of the pavement.

'Well, *au revoir*,' she said.

'No. Not *au revoir*: and you can take your affection and stuff it up your arse. I'll get another job and I'll never see you again in my life.'

He shut the door: he let in the clutch. She was not very proud of herself. Not displeased, either. 'It had to be done,' she said to herself. She was not altogether sure why.

She had passed Lucien on the stairs today at Publinf, and they had not spoken to one another. Now it was ten o'clock in the evening. She was tidying her room when she heard the phone ring and then Jean-Charles' voice, 'Laurence! Your mother wants to talk to you.'

She ran to the phone. 'Is that you, Dominique?'

'Yes. Come at once.'

'What's the matter?'

'I'll tell you.'

'I'm coming.'

Jean-Charles picked up his book again: in an irritated tone he asked, 'What's up?'

'I suppose Gilbert has told her.'

'What a to-do.'

Laurence put on her coat: she went to kiss the children.

'Why are you going out at this time of night?' asked Louise.

'Granny is rather unwell. She's asked me to buy her some medicine.'

The lift took her down to the garage, where she had parked the car she had borrowed from her father. Gilbert had told her! She reversed: drove out. Calm, keep calm. Breathe deeply several times. Keep a level head. Don't drive too fast. As luck would have it she found a place at once and pulled in to the kerb. For a moment she stood motionless at the foot of the staircase. She lacked the courage to go up, to ring the bell. What was she going to find the other side of the door? She went up the stairs; she rang.

'What's the matter?'

Dominique did not answer. Her hair was beautifully done; she was well made up; her eyes were dry; she was smoking nervously. 'Gilbert has just left,' she said, in a toneless voice. She took Laurence into the drawing-room. 'He's a swine. The biggest swine imaginable. So's his wife. But I'll stand up for myself. They want to get me down: they won't succeed.'

Laurence looked at her questioningly; she waited; when Dominique spoke the words came out slowly, clumsily. 'It's not Lucile. It's Patricia. That mentally-deficient chit. He's going to marry her.'

'Marry her?'

'Marry her. Can you imagine it? I can see it from here. A full-blown marriage at the Manoir, with orange-blossom. At the church, since it was only a civil marriage with Marie-Claire. And Lucile all of a flutter, the bride's young mama. It's killing.' She burst out laughing, her head thrown back, leaning against the back of the chair; she laughed on and on, with her eyes fixed and her face deadly pale; big sinews stood out under the skin of her throat—suddenly it was a very old woman's throat. In these cases you have to slap people or throw water in their faces, but Laurence could not bring herself to do any such thing. She only said, 'Be calm. Please, please, be calm.'

There were the dying remnants of a wood fire in the hearth: the room was too hot. The laughing stopped. Dominique's head fell forward; her face collapsed. Talk.

'Does Marie-Claire agree to a divorce?'

'Only too delighted: she hates me. I imagine she'll be at the party.' Dominique brought her fist down on the arm of her chair. 'I've struggled all my life. And at twenty that silly little cunt is going to be the wife of one of the richest men in France. She'll still be young when he kicks the bucket, leaving her half his money. Do you think that's justice?'

'Oh, as for justice ... You succeeded all by yourself, and that's something terrific. You didn't need anyone. That proves your size. Show them you're strong and that you don't give a damn about Gilbert ...'

'You think it's terrific to succeed on your own? You don't know what it means. What you have to do, what you have to put up with; above all when you're a woman. I've been humiliated all my life long. With Gilbert ...' Dominique's voice wavered. 'With Gilbert I felt I was protected: at peace at last, after all those years ...'

She said that in such a tone that Laurence felt a sudden impulse towards her. Safety: peace. It seemed to her that she was in contact with the underlying truth, the truth of a life that was so desperately eager to find disguises.

'Darling, you ought to be proud of yourself. And don't feel humiliated any more, never any more. Forget Gilbert: he's not worth regretting. Of course it's hard, and of course it will need a little time, but you'll overcome these feelings...'

'It's not humiliating, to be scrapped like a bit of old junk? Oh, I can just hear them laughing.'

'There's nothing to laugh about.'

'Still, they'll laugh all right.'

'Then they're fools. Take no notice of them.'

'But I can't. You don't understand. You're like your father—you float above it all. But for me, these are the people I live with.'

'Don't see them any more.'

'Then who am I going to see?' Tears began to run down Dominique's pallid face. 'It's bad enough being old. But I told myself that Gilbert would be there—that he would always be there. And now he's gone. Old and alone: it's appalling.'

'You aren't old.'

'I soon shall be.'

'You aren't alone. You have me; you have us.'

Dominique wept. There was a flesh and blood woman with a heart under all those disguises, a woman who felt age coming on and who was terrified by loneliness: she whispered 'A woman without a man is a woman entirely alone.'

'You'll meet another man. Meanwhile you have your job.'

'My job? Do you think that means anything to me? It did once, because I wanted to succeed. Now I have succeeded, and I wonder just what I've succeeded at.'

'Exactly what you wanted to succeed at. You've got a terrific job—you do extraordinarily interesting work.'

Dominique was not listening. Her eyes were fixed on the wall opposite her: a successful woman! Very impressive at a distance. But when you are alone in your bedroom at night ... wholly, finally alone. She shivered, as though she were coming out of a trance. I shall not put up with it! I shall not bear it! 'You bear things; you bear them,' said Gilbert. True or false?

'Travel. Go to Baalbek without him.'

'Alone?'

'With another woman, a friend.'

'Do you know any woman who is a friend of mine? And where am I going to find the money? I don't even know if I shall be able to keep Fueverolles: it's a very expensive place to run.'

'Take your car and drive down to Italy: give yourself a complete change.'

'No! No! I shan't give in. I'll do something.'

Dominique's face had grown so hard again that Laurence was obscurely frightened. 'What? What can you do?'

'At all events I shall have my revenge.'

'How do you mean?'

Dominique paused: a kind of smile twisted her mouth. 'I'm sure they've kept the girl in ignorance of her mother's whoring with Gilbert. I'll tell her. And how he used to talk about Lucile—her breasts down to her knees and all the rest.'

'You'd never do that! It would be madness. You'd never go and see her!'

'No. But I can write to her.'

'You're not speaking seriously?'

'Why not?'

'It would be revolting!'

'And what they're doing, that's not revolting, I suppose? Fair play, doing the handsome thing—what stuff! They've no right to make me suffer. I'm not going to return good for evil.'

Laurence had never judged Dominique; she never judged anybody. But she shivered. It was so dark in that heart; there were serpents writhing in it. Prevent that at all costs.

'It'll get you nowhere. You'll lower yourself in their eyes and the marriage will still take place.'

'That I doubt,' said Dominique. She thought; she weighed things up. 'Patricia is a ninny. That's just like Lucile: you have lovers, but Baby doesn't know anything about it, Baby's a virgin, Baby deserves her orange-blossom...'

Laurence was dumbfounded by Dominique's sudden vulgarity. Never had she spoken in this voice, in this horrible way: it was some other woman speaking, not Dominique. 'So when this Child of Mary learns the truth, I reckon she'll have quite a shock.'

'She's never done anything to you; it's not her.'

'It's her too.' In an aggressive voice Dominique added, 'What are you defending them for?'

'I'm defending you against yourself. You always told me that one has to be able to take it—to put up with dreadful blows. You so despised Jeanne Texcier.'

'But I'm not killing myself: I'm taking my revenge.'

What to say? What argument to put forward? 'They'll say you're lying.'

'She'll not tell them anything. She'll hate them too much.'

'Suppose she does speak to them. They'll tell everybody you've written these letters.'

'Not a bit of it. They aren't going to wash their dirty linen in public.'

'They'll say you have written base, filthy letters, without being explicit.'

'I'll be explicit, all right.'

'Can you imagine what people will think of you?'

'They'll think I don't let myself be shoved around. In any case I'm a woman who's been ditched—an old woman ditched in favour of a girl. I'd rather be hateful than ridiculous.'

'I beg you...'

'Oh, you make me tired,' said Dominique. 'All right, I

99

shan't do it. There!' Once more her face came to pieces and she burst out sobbing. 'I've never had any luck. Your father was no good. No good at all. And when at last I do meet a man, a real man, he throws me over for an idiot aged twenty.'

'Would you like me to stay the night?'

'No. Give me my pills. I'll increase the dose a little and I'll sleep. I'm all in.'

A glass of water, a green capsule, two little white tablets. Dominique swallowed them. 'You can leave me now.'

Laurence kissed her mother and closed the front door behind her. She drove slowly. Was Dominique going to write that letter or not? How to stop her? Warn Gilbert? That would be a betrayal. And he could not keep a watch on Patricia's mail. Take Mama off on a voyage at once, starting tomorrow? She would refuse. What to do? As soon as that question comes up what utter confusion! I've always run along a set of rails. I've never decided anything; not even my marriage, nor my profession, nor my affair with Lucien—that came and went in spite of me. Things happen to me, that's all. What to do? Ask Jean-Charles' advice?

'Oh Lord above, if you knew what a state Dominique was in,' she said. 'Gilbert has told her everything.'

He put down his book, having carefully marked his place. 'It was to be expected.'

'I had hoped she'd stand up to it better. All this last month she's been telling me such awful things about Gilbert.'

'There is so much involved. The lolly, for one thing: she'll have to change her style of living.'

Laurence stiffened. All right, so Jean-Charles loathed pathos: but even so, such indifference in his voice!

'Dominique doesn't love Gilbert for his money.'

'But he's got it and that counts. It counts for everybody, you know,' he said aggressively.

She did not reply, but went to her room. Obviously he's

100

not got over the eight hundred thousand francs that the accident is going to cost him. And he's holding me responsible for it! She snatched off her clothes. Anger was rising up inside her. I won't let myself get angry: I must sleep well. A glass of water, some exercises, a cold shower. Obviously I couldn't rely on Jean-Charles for advice: get involved in other people's affairs—never. There was only one person who could help Laurence and that was her father. And after all, in spite of his understanding and his generosity, she was not going to go and urge him to weep over Dominique's disappointments. For once she took a pill before getting into bed. Too many emotions altogether since Sunday: everything always happens at once.

She was afraid of waking her mother, so she kept herself from telephoning until it was time to leave for the office. 'How are you?' she asked. 'Did you sleep?'

'Splendidly, until four this morning.' There was a kind of exciting challenge in Dominique's voice.

'Only until four?'

'Yes. I woke up at four.' There was a pause and then in a triumphant tone Dominique said, 'I wrote to Patricia.'

'Oh no! No!' Laurence's heart began beating furiously. 'You haven't sent the letter?'

'By express, at five o'clock. I laugh and I laugh and I laugh when I think of her face, the poppet.'

'Dominique! That's insane! She mustn't read that letter. Phone her: beg her not to open it.'

'Phone her? Don't be silly. Anyhow, it's too late. She's read it by now.'

Laurence said nothing. She hung up and she just had time to reach the bathroom: a spasm wrenched her stomach and she vomited all the tea she had just drunk. It had not happened to her for years, being sick from emotion. Her stomach was empty but it went on heaving violently. She had no clear visual image: she could not picture Patricia or Lucile or Gilbert: she could see nothing. But she was afraid. Wildly, irrationally afraid. She drank a glass of water and returned to let herself flop on a divan.

'Are you unwell, Mama?' asked Catherine.

'Just a little. It's nothing much. Go and do your homework.'

'Are you unwell or are you sad? Is it because of Granny?'

'Why do you ask that?'

'Just now you told me she was better; but you didn't seem to believe it.'

Catherine lifted an anxious but trusting face up to her mother. Laurence put her arm round the child and pressed her to her side.

'She's not really ill. Only she was going to marry Gilbert and now he doesn't love her any more—he's going to marry someone else. So she's unhappy.'

'Oh.' Catherine thought. 'What can we do?'

'Be very kind to her. Nothing else.'

'Mama, will Granny grow wicked?'

'How do you mean?'

'Brigitte says that when people are wicked it's because they are unhappy. Except the Nazis.'

'She told you that?' Laurence squeezed Catherine tighter. 'No. Granny won't grow wicked. But take care when you see her: don't look as though you knew she was unhappy.'

'I wish you weren't unhappy either, so I do,' said Catherine.

'I'm happy because I have such a very good, kind little daughter. Go and do your homework and don't tell Louise anything about all this: she's too young. Promise?'

'I promise,' said Catherine. She dabbed a kiss on her mother's cheek and went off looking pleased. A child: so affectionate, so whole-hearted. Must she turn into a woman like me, with stones in her bosom and the reek of sulphur in her head?

'Don't let's think about it: I don't want to think about it any more,' said Laurence inwardly as she sat there in her office at Publinf, talking over the launching of Floribelle cambric. Half-past eleven. Patricia must have had the express by eight o'clock.

'Are you listening to what I say?' asked Lucien.

'Of course I am.'

He was fixed in resentment and hostility; she would rather not have seen him at all, but Voisin would not let him go. The innocence of cambric, its sophisticated innocence; its transparent quality; the crystal clarity of springs but roguish daring too—those were the contrasts to be worked upon. The telephone bell made Laurence jump. Gilbert: 'I very strongly advise you to go and see your mother.' A harsh, cruel voice. He hung up. Laurence dialled her mother's number. She hated this machine that made people so close and so remote; a Cassandra whose harsh voice broke abruptly into one's day—the mouthpiece of disaster. Far away the bell throbbed in the silence: you would have said the flat was empty. But from Gilbert's words Dominique must be there. Somebody in an empty flat—what did that mean? A body.

'My mother has had an accident. A stroke—I don't know what. I'm going to run over to her place.' She must have looked very strange: neither Lucien nor Mona said a word.

She ran: she got into her car and drove as fast as she could; she abandoned it on the no-parking side and ran up the stairs four at a time, too impatient to bring down the lift; she rang double rings three times. Silence. She kept her finger hard on the button.

'Who is it?'

'Laurence.'

The door opened. But Dominique kept her back turned: she was wearing her blue dressing-gown. She went into her bedroom, where the curtains were still drawn. In the gloom Laurence could make out a vase overturned on the floor, tulips scattered here and there, a pool of water on the carpet. Dominique flung herself into a low armchair. It was like the day before: with her head thrown back and her eyes fixed on the ceiling, she wept with great sobs that swelled her sinewy neck. The front of the dressing-gown was ripped; buttons torn off. 'He hit me.'

Laurence went into the bathroom and opened the medicine cupboard. 'You haven't taken a tranquillizer? No? Then swallow that.'

Dominique obeyed. And she talked, speaking in a voice that belonged to no one. Gilbert had rung the bell at ten o'clock; she had thought it was the concierge and she had opened the door. Straight away Patricia had gone to weep in Gilbert's arms, Lucile shrieked, he kicked the door to behind him, stroked Patricia's hair very lovingly and soothed her, and then there in the hall he had insulted Dominique and slapped her; he had gripped her by the collar of her blue dressing-gown and dragged her into the bedroom. Dominique choked. 'There's nothing left but to die,' she gasped.

What had happened exactly? Laurence's mind was in a blaze of confusion. Behind the disorder of the unmade bed, the torn dressing-gown, the flowers thrown about, she could see Gilbert, with his plump, manicured hands, and that wickedness on his rather too fat face. Had he dared? What was there to have stopped him? Horror seized Laurence by the throat, horror at what had taken place in Dominique's heart during those few moments, and at what was happening there now. Oh, all the pictures had been shattered to pieces, and it would never be possible to put them together again. Laurence wanted to take a tranquillizer too: she needed all her clarity of mind.

'What a swine,' she said. 'They are utter swine.'

'I want to die,' whispered Dominique.

'Come! Don't sit there weeping—it would give him too much satisfaction,' said Laurence. 'Wash your face, have a shower, dress and let's get out of here.'

Gilbert had grasped that there was only one way of piercing Dominique to the very heart—humiliation. Would she ever recover from it? How easy it would be if Laurence could take her in her arms and stroke her hair as she would have done with Catherine. What she found so terribly distressing was the revulsion that was mixed with her pity—it was as though she were sorry for an injured toad; sorry, but unable to bring herself to touch it. Gilbert was abhorrent to her; but so too was her mother.

'At this very minute he's telling Patricia and Lucile all about it.'

'Of course he's not. Knocking a woman about—there's nothing to be proud of in that.'

'He's proud of it: he'll boast about it all over the place. I know him...'

'He could never give his reasons. You told me so yesterday—he's not going to shout from the housetops that he went to bed with his fiancée's mother.'

'The filthy little bitch! She showed him my letter!'

Laurence stared at her mother in amazement. 'But Dominique, I told you she would show it to him!'

'I didn't believe it. I thought she would be utterly disgusted and break things off. That's what she ought to have done, out of respect for her mother—say nothing and break. But she wants Gilbert's money.'

For years and years she had treated people as obstacles to be overcome; and she had overcome them. She had ended by no longer knowing that others existed in their own right, no longer understanding that they would not necessarily fall in with her plans. Set and obstinate in her hysterias and her play-acting. Always imitating someone because she was unable to originate conduct suited to a particular set of circumstances. And she was thought to be a capable, self-possessed, efficient woman...

'Put your clothes on,' repeated Laurence. 'Wear dark glasses and I'll take you to have lunch somewhere—somewhere outside Paris where we shall be certain of meeting no one.'

'I'm not hungry.'

'It will do you good to eat.'

Dominique went into the bathroom. The tranquillizer had worked. She washed in silence. Laurence threw out the flowers, mopped up the water, telephoned her office. She put her mother in the car. Dominique did not speak. The big sunglasses accentuated the paleness of her skin.

Laurence chose a restaurant that was almost all glass, a place perched on a height that looked out over a huge suburban landscape. There was a big party going on at the far end of the room. An expensive place, but not fashionable; Dominique's acquaintances did not go there. They picked a table.

'I must tell my secretary I'm not coming in today,' said Dominique.

She walked off, her shoulders a little bowed. Laurence went out on to the terrace that overlooked the plain. Far off the whiteness of the Sacré Cœur and the slates of the roofs of Paris gleamed under a deep blue sky. It was one of those days when the happiness of spring thrusts up through the December chill. There were birds singing in the naked trees. Along the motorway beneath her the cars sped by, glittering as they went. She stood there motionless: time had suddenly come to a stop. Behind this planned, built-up landscape, with its roads, its great blocks, its housing-estates, its hurrying motor cars, there was something showing through, something whose approach was so moving that she forgot all these worries, all these plots, everything: she was nothing but a timeless waiting, an expectancy with neither beginning nor end. The birds sang, heralding the rebirth still far away. A pink haze formed along the horizon and for a long pause she stood there, unmoving, gripped by a mysterious excitement. Then there she was again on a restaurant terrace; she was cold and she went back to her table.

Dominique sat down beside her. Laurence passed her the menu.

'I don't want anything.'

'Never mind. Choose something.'

'Choose for me.' Dominique's lips trembled; she looked quite worn out. Her voice sank to humility. 'Laurence, don't talk about this to anybody. I don't want Marthe to know. Nor Jean-Charles. Nor your father.'

'Of course not.'

Laurence felt a lump in her throat. Her heart went out to her mother: she did so want to help her. But how?

'If only you knew what he said to me! It's horrible. He's a horrible man.' Two tears flowed behind the dark glasses.

'Don't think about it any more. Forbid yourself to think about it.'

'I can't.'

'Go away—travel somewhere. Take a lover. And make a fresh start.'

Laurence ordered omelette, sole, and a white wine. She knew that before her there lay hours and hours of going over and over the same thing again and again. She made up her mind to that. But eventually she would have to leave Dominique. And what then?

Dominique made a sly, mad sort of a face. 'At least I think I've rather spoilt their wedding-night for them,' she said.

'I should like to find something really stunning for the Dufrènes,' said Jean-Charles.

'We'll have to look in Papa's part of the world.'

Jean-Charles had a special heading in their budget for presents, tips, going out, parties and unforeseen expenses, and he checked it with the same attention to due proportion and balance as he did the others. They were going to buy their presents that afternoon, and what they would spend would by then have been fixed to within a few thousand francs. A tricky job. It must neither look mean nor too splashy; and the present must reflect not this desire for moderation but solely the wish to give its recipient pleasure. Laurence ran her eye over the figures that her husband was writing. 'Five thousand francs for Goya isn't much.'

'She's only been with us three months. She can't be given as much as if she had worked the whole year.'

Laurence was silent. She would take ten thousand francs of her own money: it was convenient, having a job where they gave you bonuses that your husband knew nothing about. It prevented arguments. There was no point in upsetting Jean-Charles: Catherine's report was not going to please him at all. Still, she must make herself show it. 'The children brought their term's reports back yesterday.' She passed him Louise's. First, third, second. Jean-Charles glanced at it indifferently. 'Catherine's is not quite so good.'

He looked at it and his face darkened: twelfth in French, ninth in Latin, eighth in mathematics, fifteenth in history, third in English. 'Twelfth in French! She used always to be first! What's the matter with her?'

'She doesn't like her teacher.'

'And fifteenth in history, ninth in Latin!'

The remarks did not help at all: 'Could do better. Talks in class. Absent-minded.' Absent-minded: does she get that from me?

'Have you been to see her teachers?'

'I've seen the history-mistress: Catherine looks tired and she's either wool-gathering or else she's noisy and plays the fool. Girls often go through a crisis at that age, she told me—it's the coming of puberty. There's no need to worry too much.'

'It looks a pretty serious crisis to me. She doesn't work and she cries at night.'

'She's cried twice.'

'That's twice too often. Call her: I want to speak to her.'

'Don't scold her. Her marks aren't catastrophic, after all.'

'You're easily satisfied!'

In the children's room Catherine was helping Louise make transfers. She had been sweetly kind to her little sister ever since she had wept for jealousy. There's nothing to be done about it, thought Laurence: Louise is pretty, a funny, cute little creature; but Catherine's the one I prefer. Why has her work gone off like this? Laurence had her own ideas upon the subject, but she was quite determined to keep them to herself.

'Sweetie, Papa wants to see you. He's worried about your report.'

Catherine followed her in silence, her head rather low. Jean-Charles looked at her sternly. 'Come now, Catherine, tell me what's the matter with you. Last year you were always in the first three.' He held the report in front of her eyes. 'You don't work.'

'Oh, I do.'

'Twelfth, fifteenth!'

She looked up at her father with astonishment. 'What does that matter?'

'Don't be impertinent!'

Laurence broke in, speaking cheerfully. 'If you want to be a doctor, you have to work hard.'

'Oh, I shall work: that will interest me,' said Catherine. 'At present they never talk about things I find interesting.'

'History, literature—you don't find them interesting?' asked Jean-Charles in a righteous voice.

In any disagreement he was always more concerned with being right than with understanding the other person: otherwise he would have asked, 'What do you find interesting?' Catherine would not have been able to reply, but Laurence knew—it was the world around her, the world that was hidden from her but that she could see in odd glimpses. 'Is it your friend Brigitte who makes you talk in class?'

'Oh, Brigitte, she's very good at lessons.' Catherine's voice grew warmer. 'She has bad marks in French, because the teacher's stupid, but she was first in Latin and third in history.'

'Well then, you ought to copy her. It makes me very sad to think of my little daughter turning into a dunce.'

Tears welled up in Catherine's eyes, and Laurence stroked her hair. 'She'll work better next term. Now she's going to make the most of the holidays and forget school. Run along, sweetie; go and play with Louise.'

Catherine left the room and in a vexed tone Jean-Charles said, 'If you pet her every time I scold her, there's no point in my bothering.'

'She's so sensitive.'

'Too sensitive. What's the matter with her? She cries, she asks questions that aren't suitable for her age, and she no longer works.'

'You said yourself that she was of the age to ask questions.'

'All right. But this falling-off in her school work is abnormal. I wonder whether it's good for her to have a friend who's older than she is and a Jewess into the bargain.'

'What?'

'Don't take me for an anti-Semite. But it's known that Jewish children are rather disturbingly precocious and extremely emotional.'

'Oh, that's just talk: I don't believe it for a minute. Brigitte is precocious because she has no mother and therefore has to manage all by herself, and because she has a big brother she is very much attached to. In my opinion she has an excellent influence upon Catherine: the child is growing more mature, she's thinking, enlarging her mind. You attach too much importance to doing well at school.'

'I want my daughter to be a success in life. Why don't you take her to see a psychologist?'

'Certainly not! Are people to go and consult a psychologist every time a child slips a few places in class?'

'Slips places in class and cries at night. Why not? Why

should you refuse to go and see a specialist when there's emotional trouble, since you take your daughters to a physician the moment they cough?'

'I don't like that idea in the very least.'

'Of course you don't—that's the stock reaction. The parents are automatically jealous of the psychologists who look after their children. But we are intelligent enough to go beyond that. You're odd. In some ways you're quite modern and in others downright backward.'

'Backward or not, I think Catherine's fine as she is: I don't want anyone to wreck her for me.'

'A psychologist won't wreck her. He'll only try to see what it is that's not running smoothly.'

'Running smoothly—what's that supposed to mean? In my opinion things don't run so very smoothly with the people you think of as normal. If Catherine is interested in things outside her school programme, that doesn't mean she's off her head.'

Laurence had spoken with a violence that she herself found surprising. Follow your own little road without straying an inch: looking to the right or the left will be prosecuted; each age brings its own tasks; if you are overcome by anger drink a glass of water and do some exercises. It's worked for me, it's worked very well indeed; but nobody's to make me bring up Catherine in the same way. She said vehemently, 'I shan't prevent Catherine from reading books she likes nor from seeing friends she's fond of.'

'You must admit that she's lost a great deal of her steadiness. Your father was right for once—knowledge is a splendid thing, but it is dangerous for children. We must take precautions and perhaps shelter her from certain influences. There's no point in her learning the unhappy things of life right away. The time for that will come later.'

'That's what you think! It never is the time and it never will be the time,' said Laurence. 'Mona's dead right when she says we understand nothing. Every day we read

111

hideous things in the papers, and we go right on ignoring them.'

'Oh, don't start another guilty-conscience scene, like the one you treated me to in '62,' said Jean-Charles sharply.

Laurence felt herself go pale: it was as though he had hit her in the face. She had been trembling, quite beside herself, that day when she read the account of that woman tortured to death. Jean-Charles had taken her in his arms, and full of trust she had let herself go while he said, 'It's appalling'—she had believed that he was moved too. Because of him she had calmed down and she had done her best to expel the memory, very nearly succeeding. It was mainly because of him that she had given up reading the papers from then onwards. And in fact he had not given a damn; he had said 'It's appalling' just to soothe her: and now here he was throwing the incident in her teeth with a kind of malignance. What a betrayal! So sure of his rights, so furious if we disturb the picture he has made of us, the exemplary little daughter and the exemplary young wife, and utterly indifferent to what we are in reality.

'I don't want Catherine to inherit your easy conscience.'

Jean-Charles thumped the table; he had never been able to bear opposition. 'You're the one who's throwing her off the rails, with your scrupulosity—your sentimentality.'

'Me, sentimentality?'

She was honestly amazed. She had been sentimental once: but Dominique and then Jean-Charles had thoroughly smothered that. Mona blamed her for her indifference and Lucien for having no heart.

'Yes, and the other day we had it all over again with that cyclist . . .'

'Get out,' said Laurence. 'Or I'll go myself.'

'I'll go. I have to see Monnod. But it wouldn't be a bad idea if you went to see a psychologist on your own account,' said Jean-Charles, getting up.

She shut herself in her room. Drink a glass of water; do exercises: no. This time she let herself go in fury: a hurricane tore through her bosom, shaking her to the core—a physical pain, but at least she could feel herself living. She saw herself again sitting on the edge of the bed and she heard Jean-Charles' voice, 'It really doesn't seem very clever to me: we only have a third-party-collision insurance. Everybody would have given evidence in your favour.' And in a flash she realized that he was not joking. He was blaming me—he blames me still—for not having saved him eight hundred thousand francs by taking the risk of killing a man. The front door shut: he had gone. Would he have done it? At all events he's angry with me for not having done it.

For a long while she sat there, her head burning and an oppressive weight on the back of her neck; she would have liked to cry—since when had she forgotten how to?

There was a record playing in the children's room— old English songs: Louise was doing transfers, Catherine reading *Lettres de mon Moulin*. She looked up. 'Mama, was Papa very cross?'

'He doesn't understand why you don't work as well as you used to.'

'You're cross too.'

'No. But I do wish you would make an effort.'

'Papa is often cross these days.'

Yes: there had been the arguments with Vergne and then the accident—he had been angry when the children had tried to make him tell them about it. Catherine had noticed his ill-temper; she was obscurely aware of Dominique's unhappiness and Laurence's anxiety. Was that the reason for her nightmares? In fact she had cried out three times.

'He has worries. The car has to be replaced, and that costs a lot. And then although he's happy to have changed jobs, it does mean a lot of difficulties.'

'It's sad to be a grown-up,' said Catherine in a tone of

certainty.

'Oh no; there are lovely things about being grown-up—for example having nice little daughters like you two.'

'Papa doesn't think I'm such a nice little daughter.'

'He does really. If he weren't so fond of you he wouldn't mind at all if you had bad marks.'

'Do you really think so?'

'Of course I do.'

Was Jean-Charles right? Does she get this anxious nature from me? It's frightening to think that you mark your children merely by being yourself. A stab to the heart. Anxiety, remorse. Everyday little fits of temper, the chance of a word, of a silence, all these fortuitous trifles that ought to vanish behind me are written deep in the mind of this child, who will turn them over and who will remember them just as I remember the exact tones of Dominique's voice. It seems unfair. You can't assume the responsibility for everything you do—or don't do. 'What do you do for them?' These accounts suddenly and insistently called for in a world where nothing really matters much. It was like a huge mistake.

'Mama,' said Louise, 'will you take us to see the crèche?'

'Yes. Tomorrow or the day after.'

'Could we go to midnight mass? Pierrot and Riquet say that it's so beautiful, with music and lights.'

'We'll see.'

So many facile, glib fables to soothe the young: Fra Angelico's paradise, the wonders of tomorrow, solidarity, charity, help for the underdeveloped countries. Some of them I reject; others I more or less accept.

A ring at the bell: a bouquet of red roses with Jean-Charles' card: 'With love.' She took out the pins, undid the shiny paper: she felt like throwing them in the dustbin. A bouquet is always something more than mere flowers—it's friendship, it's hope, gratitude, happiness. Red roses—glowing love. And that was just what it was not. Not even sincere regret, she was sure of that: only a gesture towards the conventions of married life—no disagreements over Christmas. She arranged the roses in a glass vase. It was no flaming outburst of voluptuous passion; but they were lovely: and although they had been made to bring a lying message they were not to blame for it.

Laurence brushed the scented petals with her lips. What do I really think of Jean-Charles at the very bottom of my mind? What does he think of me? She had the feeling that none of this was of the least importance. In any case we are tied together for life. Why Jean-Charles rather than anyone else? That was how things were. (Some other young wife, hundreds of young wives, were at that very moment wondering why him rather than anyone else.) Whatever he did or said, whatever she said or did, there would be no penalty. There was no point even in feeling angry. No remedy whatever.

As soon as she heard the key in the lock she ran to meet him, she said thank you, they kissed. He was beaming with joy because Monnod had entrusted him with a plan for prefabricated dwellings on the outskirts of Paris, a certain and very profitable piece of business. He lunched quickly (she said that she had eaten with the children: she could not swallow a thing) and they set off in a cab to buy their presents. They walked along the rue du faubourg Saint-Honoré: the day was fine, dry and cold. The shop-windows were lit up; there were Christmas-trees in the street and in the shops; men and women hurried along or strolled by, carrying their parcels, smiling. They say it's lonely people who don't like Christmas and the other holidays: I'm as unsolitary as can be, but I don't like them either. The Christmas-trees, the parcels, the smiles—they made her feel uncomfortable.

'I want to give you a very splendid present,' said Jean-Charles.

'Don't do anything wild. With that car to replace...'

'Don't talk about that any more. I want to do something wild, and since this morning I can.'

The windows slowly went by one after another. Scarves, clips, chain-bracelets, jewels for millionaires—a diamond and ruby choker, a long rope of black pearls, sapphires, emeralds, gold bracelets, bracelets made of precious stones—more modest toys, rock crystal, jade, rhinestones, glass bubbles with brilliant ribbons inside them, twirling in the light, blown glass bottles, thick crystal vases for a single rose, white and blue opaline jars, china bottles, bottles made of lacquer, gold powder-compacts, others inlaid with jewels; scent, lotions, atomizers, feather waistcoats, pale pullovers made of wool and camel hair, the frothy coolness of the underclothes, the softness, the downy softness of the housecoats in pastel shades, the richness of lameé, cloqué, brocade, gaufré, the filmy woollens frosted with metallic threads, the muted red of Hermès' window, the contrast of leather and fur in which each set off the other, clouds of swansdown, foaming lace. And all those eyes shining with desire to possess, the men's as well as the women's.

My eyes used to shine like that: I loved going into the shops, gazing at the flowers: through my hands there used to flow the softness of mohair and angora, the coolness of linen, the charm of lawn and the sensuous warmth of velvet. It was because she loved these abodes of Paradise, carpeted with luxurious materials and planted with carbuncle-bearing trees that she had been able to talk about them right away. And now she was the victim of the slogans she herself had invented. Vocational deformation: as soon as I am attracted to a setting or an object I wonder what motivation I am obeying. She scented the humbug; and all these pretences and subtleties tired her—in the end, indeed, they angered her. I shall finish by becoming detached from everything ... Nevertheless she stopped in front of a suède jacket of a colour without a name—the colour of mist, of time, of fairy-tales.

'What a lovely thing.'

'Buy it. But that's not my present. I want to give you

something wholly useless.'

'No, I don't want to buy it.'

The urge had left her already: the jacket would no longer have the same shade nor the same velvety texture once it was no longer next to the three-quarter length coat the colour of dead leaves, no longer among the smooth leather overcoats and the brilliant scarves that surrounded it in the window: it was the whole display that one coveted through each of its component objects.

She pointed to a camera shop. 'Let's go in there. That's what would give Catherine most pleasure.'

'Of course, there's no question of her having no presents,' said Jean-Charles in a preoccupied tone. 'But I do assure you we shall have to do something.'

'I promise you I'll think about it.'

They bought a camera that was easy to work. There was a green signal to show when the light was right: if it was not, it turned red. Impossible to get it wrong. Catherine would be pleased. But it's something else that I should like to give her: security, a happy mind, the joy of being alive. I claim to be selling these things when I launch a product. All lies. In the shop-window the things still retain the halo that surrounded them in the glossy picture. But when you have them in your hands you no longer see anything but a lamp, an umbrella, a camera. Lifeless: cold.

There were a great many people in Manon Lescaut's—women, a few men, some couples. These last were young married pairs; they gazed lovingly at one another while he settled a bracelet on his wife's wrist. With shining eyes Jean-Charles put a necklace round Laurence's throat. 'Do you like it?' It was an enchanting necklace, discreetly brilliant; but far too rich, far too costly. She stiffened. Jean-Charles would never have given it to me but for this morning's quarrel. It's an amends, a symbol, a surrogate. Of what? Of something that no longer exists and which perhaps never did exist—a warm, exceedingly close link that should make all presents unnecessary.

'It suits you extraordinarily well!' said Jean-Charles.

Doesn't he feel the weight of the unsaid things between us? Not the weight of silence but of the empty phrases: isn't he aware of the remoteness, the absence, underneath the politeness of the ritual gestures?

She took it off with a kind of fury: as if she were freeing herself from a lie. 'No! I don't want it.'

'You just said that that was the one you liked best.'

'Yes,' She smiled faintly. 'But it's too extravagant.

'As for that, I'm the one who decides,' he said, displeased. 'But still, if you don't like it, let's leave it.'

She picked up the necklace again: what was the point of crossing him? Might as well have done with it.

'It's not that; I think it's wonderful. I only thought it would be rather wild. But after all that's your business.'

'Yes, that's my business.'

She bowed her head a little so that he could fasten the necklace again: a perfect picture of the couple who still adore one another after ten years of marriage. He was buying conjugal peace, the delights of the home, understanding, love; and pride in himself. She gazed at herself in the mirror. 'Darling, you were right to insist: I'm wild with happiness.'

According to custom the New Year's Eve party was held at Marthe's: 'It's the housewife's privilege; I have all my time free,' she said, complacently. Hubert and Jean-Charles split the cost: there was often friction because Hubert was close-fisted (to be sure he was not rolling in money) and Jean-Charles did not choose to pay more than his brother-in-law. The year before the supper had been quite pitiful. It would be passable this evening, thought Laurence, having inspected the buffet set up at the far end of the drawing-room, which Marthe had Christmasified with candles, a little tree, mistletoe, holly, angels' hair and coloured glass balls. Their father had brought four bottles of champagne that he had from a friend who lived in Rheims, and Dominique had provided an immense foie gras from Périgord—'So much better than the Strasburg foie gras—the best anywhere in France.' What with that and the braised beef, the rice salad, the little cocktail things, the fruit, the petits fours, the bottles of wine and whisky, there would be plenty to eat and drink for ten people.

Other years Dominique had spent the Christmas and New Year with Gilbert. It was Laurence who had had the idea of asking her this evening. She had said to her father, 'Would it irk you much? She is so very much alone, so unhappy.'

'I don't mind in the very least.'

No one knew the details but everyone was aware of the break. There were the Dufrènes, brought by Jean-Charles, and Henri and Thérèse Vuillenot, who were friends of Hubert's. Dominique was very much 'family party', she was dressed in the character of 'youthful grandmother' in a discreet honey-coloured jersey dress, her hair nearer white than blonde. She smiled gently, almost timidly, and she spoke very slowly; she was over-doing the tranquillizers—that's what gave her that numbed look. As soon as she was alone her face sagged. Laurence went over to her. 'How did you get through the week?'

'Not too badly: I slept quite well.' A mechanical smile: you would have said she was pulling at the corners of her mouth with little strings. She let the strings go. 'I've made up my mind to sell the house at Feuverolles. I can't keep up a great thing like that all on my own.'

'What a pity. If some way of managing could be found...'

'What's the point? Who am I going to entertain now? The interesting people, the Houdans, the Thiriots, the Verdelets—it was Gilbert they came for.'

'Oh, they'll come for you.'

'Do you really believe that? You don't know life yet. Socially a woman without a man counts for nothing.'

'Not you, you know. You have a name. You're some-one.'

Dominique shook her head. 'Even if she has a name a woman without a man is a half-failure, a kind of derelict ... I see how people look at me, all right it's not the same at all as it was before, believe me.'

Loneliness: it was an obsession with Dominique. Someone had put on a record; Thérèse was dancing with Hubert, Marthe with Vuillenot, Jean-Charles with Gisèle, and Dufrène asked Laurence. They all danced extremely badly.

'You're dazzling tonight,' said Dufrène.

She caught a glimpse of herself in a mirror. She was wearing a black sheath and this necklace that she did not care for. Yet it was pretty and then again it was to give her pleasure that Jean-Charles had bought it. She thought she looked commonplace. Dufrène had already drunk a certain amount, and his voice was more urgent than usual ... A pleasant fellow and a good companion for Jean-Charles (although fundamentally they were not so fond of one another as all that; indeed each was rather jealous of the other), but she had no particular liking for him.

They changed the record, they changed partners.

'Madam, may I beg the pleasure of this dance?' asked Jean-Charles.

'Charmed.'

'It's funny to see them together again!' said Jean-Charles. Laurence followed his eyes and she saw her father and Dominique sitting opposite one another, talking politely. Yes, it was funny.

'She seems to have got over it,' said Jean-Charles.

'She stuffs herself with tranquillizers, harmonizers and things like that.'

'Really, you know, they ought to take up life together again,' said Jean-Charles.

'Who?'

'Your father and mother.'

'You're out of your mind!'

'Why do you say that?'

'Their tastes are absolutely opposed. She's very sociable and he's a recluse.'

'They're both of them lonely.'

'That's nothing to do with it.'

Marthe stopped the record. 'Five to twelve!'

Hubert seized a bottle of champagne. 'I know a splendid way of uncorking champagne. It was on that programme the other day.'

'I saw it,' said Dufrène. 'But I've a trick of my own that works even better.'

'Have a go...'

They both made the cork pop out without spilling a drop and they both looked extremely proud (although each would have been even more pleased if the other had made a mess of it). They filled the glasses.

'A Happy New Year.'

'Happy New Year.'

The glasses touched: kisses, laughter, and outside the windows the huge outburst of hooters.

'What a horrible row!' said Laurence.

'They have been allowed five minutes, like children who absolutely must make a din between two classes,' said her father. 'And the people making that noise are civilized grown-ups.'

'Oh, I don't know,' said Hubert. 'It's only once a year, as the saying goes.'

They opened the other two bottles: the parcels piled up behind a sofa were brought out, the coloured string broken, the ribbons undone, the brilliantly-coloured paper printed with stars and Christmas-trees unwrapped; and everybody watched everybody else out of the corner of an eye, to see who had won in this potlatch. 'We have,' observed Laurence. For Dufrène they had found a watch that showed the time in France and all the other countries in the world; for her father an enchanting telephone, a copy of the old kind, that would go very well with his oil-lamps. Their other presents were less original, but still subtle. Dufrène had specialized in gimmicks. He gave Jean-Charles a *vénusik*—an everlasting heart that uttered seventy glops a minute—and Laurence a *motingale* that she would never dare to fix to her steering-wheel if it really did imitate the nightingale's song. Jean-Charles was delighted: he dearly loved contraptions that served no purpose, that said nothing whatever. Laurence also received gloves, scent, handkerchiefs: and everyone was enchanted, everyone cried out, thanked everyone else.

'Take plates and knives and forks and help yourselves —find yourselves places to sit,' said Marthe.

A general din; the clash of plates; it's delicious; take more than that. Laurence heard her father's voice. 'Didn't you know that? Wine must be brought to room temperature after it has been uncorked, not before.'

'It's uncommonly good.'

'It was Jean-Charles who chose it.'

'Yes, I know a very good little wine-merchant.'

Jean-Charles was capable of thinking heavily-corked wine quite delightful, but like the others he played the connoisseur. She emptied a glass of champagne. They laughed; they told jokes; and she did not think their jokes funny. The year before ... Well, she hadn't had much fun then, either, but she had gone through the motions; this year she did not feel like forcing herself—in the long run it grows wearisome. And last year she thought of Lucien: a sort of being elsewhere. Then she thought that there was someone she would have liked to be with: the regret was a little romantic flame, and it had warmed her. Not even a regret any more. Why had she decided to make this empty space in her life, to husband her time, her strength and her heart when she was by no means sure what to do with her time, her strength or her heart? Too full a life? Too empty? Full of empty things: what chaos!

'Nevertheless, you look at the pattern of several Capricorn lives and of several Gemini lives: within each group there are some disturbing analogies,' said Vuillenot.

'Scientifically it is by no means impossible that the stars should influence our lives,' said Dufrène.

'Come now! The fact of the matter is that this epoch is so drearily positive that people need the marvellous by way of compensation. They build electronic machines and they read astrological trash like *Planète*.'

Her father's vehemence delighted Laurence: he had remained so young; the youngest person there.

'That's quite true,' said Marthe. 'For my part I prefer reading the Gospel and believing in the mysteries of religion!'

'Even in religion the feeling for mystery is vanishing,' said Mme Vuillenot. 'I really find it most distressing the way they say the mass in French: and with modern music, too, into the bargain.'

'Oh, I don't agree at all,' said Marthe in her inspired voice. 'The Church must move with the times.'

'Up to a certain point.'

They moved away and in lowered voices they continued a discussion that was not for impious ears.

'Did you see the retrospective show on the television yesterday?' asked Gisèle Dufrène.

'Yes,' said Laurence. 'We seem to have lived through a pretty odd sort of year: I hadn't realized.'

'They are all like that and one never realizes,' said Dufrène.

You see the television news, the photographs in *Match*, and as you see them so you forget them. Then when you see them again all together it's rather astonishing. The bleeding corpses of whites and of Negroes; buses overturned in ravines, twenty-five children killed; others cut in two; fires; the shattered wreckage of planes; a hundred and ten passengers killed instantly; typhoons; floods; whole countries devastated; villages in flames; race-riots; local wars; the long lines of worn-out refugees. It was so dismal that in the end you almost wanted to laugh. It must be said that you watch all the disasters sitting comfortably at your own fireside and it's not true that the outside world bursts into the room: all you see is pictures, neatly framed on the little screen, pictures that do not carry their charge of reality.

'I wonder what they'll think of the film on France in twenty years' time *in* twenty years' time,' said Laurence.

'Certain aspects of it will be rather absurd, as it always happens with these things that foretell the future,' said Jean-Charles. 'But on the whole it's true.'

By way of contrast to the disasters, they had shown France in twenty years' time. The triumph of town-planning: dazzling great blocks that looked like beehives four hundred feet high, or ant-hills, all ablaze with sunlight. Motorways, laboratories, university buildings. The only snag, the commentator explained, was that the people of France might be so overcome by the weight of this abundance that they would lose all their energy. There were slow-motion pictures of lack-lustre youths who would not trouble to put one foot in front of the other. Laurence heard her father's voice. 'Generally speaking it is found that at the end of five years or even of one that the planners and the other prophets were totally wrong.'

Jean-Charles looked at him with an air of rather weary superiority. 'No doubt you are unaware that at present the foretelling of the future is becoming an exact science. Perhaps you've never heard of the Rand Corporation?'

'No.'

'It's an astonishingly well-equipped American organization. Specialists in each branch of knowledge are questioned and then the averages are taken. Thousands of scientists throughout the world take part in the work.'

His superior air irritated Laurence. 'At all events, when they tell us that people in France will lack nothing ... You don't have to consult thousands of specialists to know that in twenty years the majority still won't have bathrooms, since most of the government housing schemes only provide showers.'

She had been much shocked by this little fact when Jean-Charles had explained his plan for prefabricated dwellings to her.

'Why no bathrooms?' asked Thérèse Vuillenot.

'Plumbing is very expensive; it would put up the price of the flats,' said Jean-Charles.

'And what if the profits were cut?'

'But darling, if they were cut too much no one would have any incentive to build,' said Vuillenot.

His wife gave him an unfriendly glance. Four young couples: and who loved whom? Why should anyone love Hubert or Dufrène, why should one love anyone at all, once the first sexual blaze has gone out?

Laurence drank two glasses of champagne. Dufrène explained that in real-estate dealings it was difficult to draw a line between fraud and speculation: one was forced into illegal practices.

'But it's disturbing. What you say is very disturbing,' said Hubert. He seemed really dismayed. Laurence and her father exchanged an amused smile. 'I can't believe it,' he said. 'If one really wants to remain honest there must certainly be a way.'

'Certainly, so long as you take up another trade.'

Marthe had put on another record: they danced again. Laurence tried to teach Hubert the jerk; he worked hard, he puffed and gasped, the others watched derisively. Abruptly she stopped the lesson and went over to her father, who was arguing with Dufrène.

'"Out-of-date", that's your one word. The traditional novel—out-of-date. Humanism—out-of-date. But when I stand up for Balzac and humanism it may well be that I'm at the height of tomorrow's fashion. Nowadays you people will have nothing to do with abstract painting. So I was ahead of you ten years ago when I refused to be taken in. No. There's something over and above all these fashions: there are values; there are truths.'

She had often thought that: she had often thought

what he had just said. That is to say, I did not think it in those words, but now they had been said she recognized them for her own. Values, truths that stood out against fashion—she believed in that. But just which values, and which truths?

Abstract painting doesn't sell any more; but nor does figurative; crisis in painting; well, after all, there was such an inflation. Wearisome reiteration. Laurence was bored. I've a mind to suggest a test, she thought. You have a third-party-collison insurance and a cyclist darts straight across you: do you kill the cyclist or do you wreck the car? Which of them would honestly choose to pay eight hundred thousand francs to save the life of an unknown? Papa, obviously. Marthe? I have my doubts: in any case she is only a tool in God's hands—if He had decided to take the poor boy to Himself ... The others? If they did have the reflex of avoiding the youth I'm sure that afterwards they would regret it. 'Jean-Charles was not joking.' How many times had she repeated that to herself in the course of this week? She was still doing so. Am I the one who is abnormal? A worrier, eaten up with anxiety: what have I got that they don't have? I don't give a damn about that red-headed youth: and I should find it utterly revolting to have to run him over. That's Papa's influence. For him there's nothing that's worth a human life, although he thinks mankind a pitiful crew. And money just doesn't matter to him at all. To me it does, yes; but still less than to all the others. She listened because it was her father who was talking: tonight he was far less silent than he had been in other years.

'The castration complex! It has been so over-used to explain everything that it no longer explains anything whatever. I can just see a psychiatrist coming to attend a condemned man on the morning of his execution and finding him in tears: "What a castration complex!" he would cry.'

They laughed, and their talk flowed on. 'Are you looking for an idea? For a new product of some kind?' Her father was smiling at Laurence.

'No, I was day-dreaming. Their stories about money bore me dreadfully.'

'I know what you mean. They sincerely believe that money brings happiness.'

'It does help, of course.'

'I'm not even sure of that.' He sat down beside her. 'I don't see you any more.'

'I've spent a lot of time looking after Dominique.'

'She bombinates less than she used to.'

'That's depression.'

'And you?'

'Me?'

'How are you?'

'The holidays are tiring. Presently there will be the white sales, too.'

'You don't know what I've been thinking: we two ought to go off on a little journey together.'

'The two of us?'

An old dream that had never been realized: before, she had been too young, and then there had been Jean-Charles and the children.

'I have a holiday in February and I should like to take advantage of it to see Greece again. Couldn't you arrange things so as to be able to come with me?'

Joy like a burst of fireworks. The easiest thing in the world to get a fortnight off in February and I've got some money. But does it ever happen that a dream is realized?

'If the children are all right, if everything's all right, I could perhaps manage it. But it seems too good . . .'

'You'll try!'

'Oh of course. I'll try.'

A fortnight. At last I shall have time to ask the questions and listen to the replies that have been held over all these years. I shall know the savour of his life. I shall find out the secret that makes him so different from everybody else and from me, and that makes him capable of evoking that love that I feel for nobody but him.

'I'll do everything I can. But what about you? You won't change your mind?'

'See this is wet, and this is dry? Rot my heart if I tell a lie,' he said solemnly, as he had when she was a little girl.

CHAPTER 4

I remember one of Buñuel's films: we none of us liked it.
And yet for some time it has been haunting me. There
were people enclosed in a magic circle and they went
through a chance moment of their past lives, taking up
the thread of time and avoiding the traps into which they
had fallen before without knowing it. (Though indeed
shortly after they fell into them again.) I too should like
to go back into the past, escape the traps and succeed in
what I have failed in. What have I failed in? I don't even
know. My complaints or regrets do not form themselves into words. But this lump in my throat stops me
eating.

Let's start again. I have all the time in the world. I've
drawn the curtains. Lying down, with my eyes closed, I
shall go back over this journey picture by picture, word
by word.

The outburst of delight when he said, 'Would you like
to come to Greece with me?' I did hesitate in spite of
everything. Jean-Charles urged me to go. He thought I
was run down. And then in the end I agreed to let
Catherine see a psychologist: he thought my absence
would make their relationship easier.

'Still,' said Papa, 'it's a shame to go to Athens in a
Caravelle.' Personally I love jets. The plane shot right up
into the air and I heard it burst the walls of my prison—
my narrow life hedged in by millions of other lives of
which I knew nothing whatever. The great building
complexes and the little houses faded; I was flying over
all walls, all barriers, set free from gravity: above my
head there spread the measureless blue of space, beneath
my feet a brilliant white landscape that dazzled me and
that had no existence. I was elsewhere—nowhere and

everywhere. And my father began to talk to me about what he was going to show me and what we were going to discover together. And I thought, 'You are what I want to discover.'

The landing. The softness of the air, the smell of petrol mingled with that of the sea and pines; the pure sky, the distant hills, one of which was called Hymettus—bees foraging over the violet ground—and Papa deciphering the letters written up over the buildings: way in, way out, post office. I liked gazing at that alphabet and re-discovering the childhood mystery of the language; and I was pleased that the meaning of words and things should come to me through him, as it had in former days. 'Don't look,' he said to me on the motorway (rather dis-appointed that it had taken the place of the potholed old road of his youth.) 'Don't look: the beauty of a temple is bound up with its site: to have a true notion of its har-mony you have to see it from one particular distance and not from another. It's not as it is with cathedrals, which are just as moving—sometimes even more—from a dis-tance as they are from near at hand.' These precautions touched my heart. And indeed, perched up there on its hills, the Parthenon was just like one of those copies in false alabaster they sell in the souvenir shops. Not the slightest dash or style. But I didn't care in the very least. What mattered was that I was driving along beside Papa in that orange and grey Citroën—those Greek taxis have strange colours: blackcurrant water-ice; lemon ice-cream —with twenty days ahead of us. I walked into an hotel bedroom and I put my clothes away without having the feeling that I was playing the part of a tourist in a publicity film: everything that was happening to me was real. In the square, which looked like the terrace of one vast café, Papa ordered a drink for me, a drink made of cherries, cool, fresh, light, slightly sharp, delightfully childish. And I knew the meaning of that word you read in books: happiness. I had had a good time often enough, I had experienced pleasures, pleasure too, small triumphs, tender affection; but I knew nothing of this harmony between a blue sky and a sharp, clean taste, the past and the present united in a beloved face, and this peace within me—I knew nothing of it, except in some very far-off memories. Happiness: a justification provided for life for itself, as it were. It enfolded me as we sat there eating grilled mutton in a little restaurant. The wall of the Acropolis could be seen, bathed in an orange light, and Papa said it was sacrilege: personally I found everything delightful. I loved the medicinal taste of the resiny wine. 'You're the ideal travelling-companion,' said Papa, smiling. He smiled the next day upon the Acropolis because I listened eagerly while he explained the cyma, the drip-stone, mutule, gutta, abacus, the echinus, and the gorge of the capital; he pointed out the slight bend that softened the hardness of the horizontal lines, the lean of the vertical columns, their entasis, the subtle delicacy of the proportions. It was rather cold: beneath the pure sky a wind was blowing. Far away I could see the hills, the sea, dry little houses the colour of wholemeal bread, and Papa's voice flowed over me. I felt fine.

'The West can be blamed for a great many things,' he said. 'We have made great mistakes. But still it is in the West that man has realized and expressed himself in a way that has never had its equal.'

We hired a car; we went to see everything in the neighbourhood of Athens; and every day before sunset we went up to the Acropolis, the Pnyx or Lycabettus. Papa refused to go into the modern town. 'There's nothing to be seen there,' he told me. In the evening, on the advice of an old friend, he took me to a 'typical' little tavern—a grotto on the shore, decorated with fishing-nets, shells and hurricane-lamps. 'It's more fun than the big restaurants that your mother's so fond of.' It seemed to me just as much of a tourist-trap as any other. Instead of smoothness and comfort they sold local colour and a mild feeling of superiority over the sheep-like customers of the grand hotels. (The publicity line would have been 'be *different*', or '*different* spot'.) Papa exchanged a few words in Greek with the proprietor, and he took us—like all his customers, but each one felt singled out—into the kitchen and lifted the lids off the pots: they put much thought into their cooking. I ate heartily and without caring at all.

Marthe's voice. 'Laurence! You positively must eat something.'

'I'm asleep. Leave me alone.'

'Some broth, at least. I'm going to make you some broth.'

She's broken the thread. Where was I? The road to Delphi. I loved that dry, white landscape, the sharp breath of the wind on the summery sea; but rocks and water was all I saw—I was blind to all those things my father showed me. (His eyes, Catherine's eyes: different visions, but both full of colour, both stirring—and I blind beside them.) 'Look,' he said to me, 'that is the very crossroads where Oedipus killed Laïus.' It had happened yesterday, and it mattered very much to him. The cleft of the Pythoness, the stadium, the temples: he explained every stone: I listened, I made real efforts; in vain—the past stayed dead. And I was rather tired of being astonished, of uttering cries. The Charioteer. 'That hits you, eh?' 'Yes. It's beautiful!' I did understand what could be seen in that big green bronze man: but as for the stroke, the shock, I never felt it. I felt uneasy, even remorseful. The moments I liked best were those we spent in a little bar, talking and drinking ouzo. He told me about his journeys of long ago, and how he would have liked Dominique to go with him—and us too, as soon as we were old enough. 'To think that she has seen Bermuda and America, but neither Greece nor Italy! Still, I think she's changed for the better,' he said. 'Maybe because of that blow, that disappointment; I don't know. She is more receptive, more mature, gentler, clearer-minded.' I did not contradict him: I had no wish to deprive my poor mother of what scraps of friendship he allowed her.

Is it at Delphi that I ought to branch off to go back along the thread of time? We were sitting in a café that overhung the valley: the cold, clear night with its countless stars could be felt on the other side of the glassed-in enclosure. A little orchestra was playing; there were two couples of American tourists and a great many locals—lovers, groups of young men, families. A little girl began to dance: she was three or four, tiny, with brown hair and black eyes, a full yellow dress to her knees, white socks; she spun, her arms in the air, her face aswim with ecstasy, quite beside herself, carried away by the music, dazzled, intoxicated, transfigured, rapt. Her calm fat mother gossiped there with another heavy woman, and all the time she pushed a pram with a baby in it to and fro; she was wholly untouched by the music or the night, and from time to time she sent a cow-like gaze in the direction of the enraptured child.

'Have you seen that little girl?'

'Charming,' said Papa, quite unmoved.

A charming little girl who would turn into that maternal figure. No. I would not have it. Had I drunk too much ouzo? I too was possessed, possessed by that child who was possessed by the music. This impassioned moment would never end. The little dancer would never grow up: she would spin throughout all eternity and I should watch her. I would not have it that I should forget her, that I should once more become the young woman travelling with her father; I would not have it that one day she should look like her mother; not even remembering that she ever had been this enchanting maenad. Child condemned to death, to an appalling death with no corpse. Life was going to murder her. I thought of Catherine, whom they were murdering at that moment.

All at once I said, 'I ought never to have agreed to send Catherine to a psychologist.' Papa looked at me, surprised. No doubt Catherine had been very far away from his thoughts.

'Why are you thinking about that?'

'I often think about it. I'm worried. They forced my hand, and now I regret it.'

'I don't suppose it will do her any harm,' said Papa vaguely.

'Would you have sent me to a psychologist?'

'Certainly not.'

'Well, then.'

'But after all, I don't know: the question never arose. You were so well balanced.'

'In '45 I was pretty disorientated.'

'You had something to be disorientated about.'

'And isn't there plenty nowadays?'

'Yes: yes, I think there is. No doubt in every period it is normal to be frightened when you begin to discover the world.'

'So if she's comforted she's made abnormal.'

It was patently obvious and it bowled me over completely. On the pretext of curing Catherine of the 'sentimentalism' that worried Jean-Charles, they were going to maim her. I felt like going back the next day and taking her away from them.

'For my part, I would rather people managed on their own. I have a deep-seated feeling—don't repeat it, or they will call me an old fogey again—that all this psychology is quackery. You'll find Catherine just as you left her.'

'Do you think so?'

'I'm certain of it.'

He began talking about the excursion he had worked out for the next day. He did not take my anxiety seriously, which was natural enough. On my side I was not so wholly wrapped up in the old stones that he thought fascinating. It would have been unfair in me to have resented his attitude. No, it was not at Delphi that the line was broken.

Mycenae. Perhaps it was at Mycenae. At what exact

moment? We climbed up a stony path: the wind was raising little whirls of dust. Suddenly I saw that gate, the two headless lionesses; and I left ... was that the blow my father had been speaking about? I would sooner have called it panic. I went along the Royal Road; I saw the terraces, the great walls and the landscape that Clytemnestra had seen when she watched for the return of Agamemnon. I felt as though I had been wrenched out of myself. Where was I? I did not belong to that age when people came and went, slept and ate in this still undamaged palace. And my own life had nothing to do with these ruins. A ruin: what was it? It was neither the present nor the past; and it was not eternity either: one day no doubt it would vanish. I said to myself, 'How beautiful it is!' and I was on the verge of staggering, seized by a whirlwind, tossed about, denied, reduced to *nothing*. I should have liked to run back to the tourist office and spend the day reading thrillers. There was a group of Americans taking photographs. 'What barbarians!' said Papa. 'They take photographs so that they do not have to look.' He talked to me about the Mycenaean civilization, the splendour of the Atrides and their downfall, which Cassandra had foretold; with a guidebook in his hand he did his best to identify every inch of the ground. And I said to myself that fundamentally he was doing the same thing as the tourists he made game off: he was trying to bring these remains of an age that was not his own into his life. They would stick their photographs into an album and show them to their friends. He would carry away captioned pictures in his head and he would set them up in his private, inward museum. For my part I had neither album nor museum: I had come face to face with beauty, and I had not known what to do with it.

On the way back I said to Papa, 'I envy you.'

'Why?'

'These things mean so much to you.'

'Not to you?'

He seemed disappointed, and I hastily added, 'To me, too. But I don't understand them so well. I haven't your learning.'

'Then read the book I gave you.'

'I'll read it.'

But even when I had read it, I said to myself, I shan't be overwhelmed at the thought that the name Atreus had been found on tablets in Cappadocia. I can't suddenly feel wildly enthusiastic about these stories that are quite foreign to me. You have to have lived for years and years with Homer and the Greek tragedians; you have to have travelled a great deal; you have to be able to compare. I feel that I know nothing about these dead centuries, I have nothing to do with them, and they weigh me down intolerably.

A woman in black came out of a garden and beckoned. I went towards her: she held out her hand, stammering something. I gave her a few drachmas. I said to Papa, 'Did you see?'

'Who? The beggar?'

'She was not a beggar. She was a peasant, not even old. It's terrible, a country where the peasants beg.'

'Yes, Greece is poor,' said Papa.

When we stopped in some little town I was often tormented by the contrast between so much beauty and so much wretchedness. Once Papa had asserted that really poor communities—in Sardinia for example or Greece—attained an austere happiness, thanks to their ignorance of money and thanks to values that we have lost. But the villagers of the Peloponnese did not look in the least happy, neither the women breaking stones on the roads nor the little girls carrying buckets of water too heavy for them. But still I should have liked Papa to tell me exactly where he had met the people whose destitution made them so happy.

At Tiryns and at Epidaurus there were moments when I once more felt the emotion that had taken hold of me at Mycenae. I was very cheerful that night when we arrived at Andritsena. It was late; we had travelled by moonlight along a potholed road with a precipice on one side of it; Papa drove with a far-away look; we were both of us rather sleepy—tired and quite alone in the world in the shelter of our moving house, where the dashboard glowed gently and the headlights opened us a path through the night.

'There's a delightful hotel,' Papa told me. 'Countrified and very well run.'

It was eleven o'clock when we stopped in the village square in front of an inn with all its shutters closed.

'This isn't Kristopoulos's hotel,' he said.

'Let's look for it.'

We wandered about on foot through the little deserted streets: not a single light in the windows, no other hotel than this. Papa knocked on the door; he called out: no reply. It was very cold, and spending the night in the car would be no fun. We started shouting and knocking again. A man came running from the far end of the street: jet black hair and whiskers, dazzling white shirt.

'Are you French?'

'Yes.'

'I heard you calling in French. It's market-day tomorrow; the hotel is full.'

'You speak French very well.'

'Oh, not very. But I love France...' He smiled, a smile as dazzling as his shirt. Kristopoulos's hotel no longer existed, but he would find beds for us. We followed him: I was delighted with the adventure. It was the sort that never happens with Jean-Charles—you set off and you stop at the given time; and in any case he's always booked the rooms in advance.

The Greek knocked at a door; a woman appeared at the window. Yes, she was quite willing to let us two rooms. We thanked our guide.

'I should so much like to see you for a moment tomorrow morning, to talk about your country,' he said.

'We should be very happy. Where?'

137

'There is a café in the square.'

'Excellent. Would nine o'clock suit you?'

'Perfect.'

In my red-tiled room, under a pile of blankets, I slept right on until Papa's hand on my shoulder woke me.

'We're very lucky: it's market-day. I don't know if you are like me, but I adore markets.'

'I shall adore this one.'

The square was packed with women in black sitting behind baskets set down on the ground—eggs, goat cheese, cabbages, a few thin chickens. Our friend was waiting for us in front of the café. It was cold: the market-women must have been frozen. We went in; I was dying of hunger, but there was nothing to eat. The smell of thick black coffee comforted me.

The Greek began talking about France—he was so happy every time he met French people! How lucky we were to live in a free country! He so loved reading French books and papers. He lowered his voice, no doubt more out of habit than prudence. 'In your country nobody is put in prison for his political opinions.'

Papa's face took on a look of understanding that quite astonished me. It is true that he knows a great deal—he is so modest that one doesn't realize. 'Is the repression as harsh as ever?' he murmured.

The Greek nodded. 'The Aegina prison is full of Communists. And if you knew how they treat them!'

'Is it as terrible as in the camps?'

'Quite as terrible. But they shall not break us,' he added, rather grandiloquently.

He questioned us about the situation in France. Papa gave me a conspiratorial glance and began to talk about the difficulties of the working class, its hopes and its achievements: you would have sworn he was a Party member. It was amusing, but I was getting cramps in my stomach. I said, 'I'm going to see whether I can find something to buy.'

I wandered about the square. Other women, also

138

dressed in black, were arguing with the peasants. 'An austere happiness': it was not that at all which I read on those faces reddened with the cold. How had Papa, who was usually so clear-sighted, managed to get things so completely wrong? No doubt he had only seen these countries in the summer: they would certainly be more cheerful with the sun, with fruit and flowers.

I bought two eggs, which the proprietor of the café boiled for me. I opened one and smelt a horrible stench: I opened the other—bad too. The Greek went to fetch two others, and we had them cooked. They were both bad.

'How can they be bad? They are straight from the country.'

'The market is once a fortnight. If you are lucky you chance upon yesterday's eggs. Otherwise ... It's better to eat them hard; I ought to have warned you.'

'I would rather not eat them at all.'

A little later, on the way to the temple of Bassae, I said to Papa, 'I didn't think Greece was so poor.'

'The war ruined it, above all the civil war.'

'What a pleasant fellow that was. And you played your part very well: he's convinced that we're Communists.'

'I have a high opinion of the Communists of these parts; it is quite true that they risk prison and even their lives.'

'You knew that there were so many political prisoners in Greece?'

'Indeed I did. There was a man in the office who used to pester us to sign petitions against the Greek camps.'

'Did you sign?'

'Once, yes. As a rule I sign nothing. In the first place because it is totally useless. And then all these undertakings that look as though they are humanitarian always have political strings attached to them.'

We went back to Athens and I insisted upon seeing the modern town. We walked round the Omonia square. Dismal, ill-dressed people; a greasy smell.

'There's nothing to be seen, as you see,' said Papa. I should have liked to know what was going on behind those lack-lustre faces. In Paris too I know nothing whatever about the people who brush by me, but I'm too busy to mind; in Athens I had nothing else to do.

'We ought to know some Greeks,' I said.

'I have known some. They were not particularly attractive. Besides, nowadays the people are very much the same in every country.'

'Still, the problems here are not the same as those in France.'

'They are dreadfully commonplace, both here and there.'

For me at any rate the contrast between the wealth of the fashionable parts of the town and the sadness of the common people was far more striking than in Paris.

'I imagine this country is more cheerful in summer.'

'Greece is not cheerful,' said Papa, with a hint of reproof. 'It is beautiful.'

The Korai were beautiful, with their lips curved in a smile, their fixed gaze, their jolly and rather stupid look. I loved them. I knew that I should not forget them and I should have liked to leave the museum immediately after seeing them. I could not manage to feel any interest in the rest of the sculpture, the fragments of bas-relief, the friezes, the steles. A great weariness came over me, both bodily and spiritual: I admired Papa's power of concentration and his curiosity. In two days I was going to leave him and I knew him no better than when we had begun: I had been holding back this thought since ... when? And now it suddenly pierced me through. We had gone into a room full of vases, and I saw that there were other rooms, room after room in diminishing sequence, all full of vases. Papa settled in front of a show-case and he began to give me an account of the periods and the styles and their distinguishing features—the Homeric period, the archaic period, black-figured vases, red-figured vases, vases with a white background—and he explained

140

the scenes that were shown upon their sides. Standing there next to me he withdrew, retreated to the far end of the perspective of rooms with their shining wooden floors; or else it was I who sank down into a pit of indifference: in any case there was an unbridgeable distance between us now, because for him a varying colour or the drawing of a palm-leaf or a bird evoked astonishment and a pleasure that brought to mind his former joys, the whole of his past life. Personally I found these vases unutterably wearisome and as we paced on from case to case my boredom reached the pitch of acute distress; and at the same time I thought, 'I've failed at everything.' I stopped, saying, 'I can't go on.'

'Dear me, no. You're quite done up: you ought to have said so earlier.'

He was much upset, no doubt imagining some female weakness that had suddenly brought me to the edge of fainting. He took me back to the hotel. I drank some sherry and tried to talk to him about the Korai. But he seemed to me out of reach and disappointed.

The next morning I let him go to the Acropolis museum alone. 'I'd rather see the Parthenon again,' I said.

The air was soft: I looked at the temple and the sky and I was aware of a bitter feeling of defeat. There were parties and couples listening to the guides with a civil interest or with just-suppressed yawns. Clever advertising had made them believe that here they would be thrilled beyond all expression; and back home no one would dare to confess that he had been quite unmoved. They would urge their friends to go and see Athens and the sequence of lies would go on and on—in spite of all the disillusionments the pretty pictures would remain intact. But for all that I can still see that young couple and those two middle-aged women who were slowly going up towards the temple and talking to one another and smiling; they stopped and gazed about them with a look of easy happiness. Why not me? Why am I incapable of loving things I know to be worthy of love?

Marthe came into the room. 'I've made you some broth.'

'I don't want any.'

'Make yourself take a little.'

To please them Laurence swallowed some. She had not eaten for two days. What of it, since she was not hungry? Their anxious looks. She finished the cup; her heart began to beat and she came out in a sweat all over. Just time to get into the bathroom to be sick, like the day before yesterday and the day before that. What a relief! She would have liked to empty herself even more completely, vomit her whole being right out. She rinsed her mouth and dropped on to her bed, exhausted, calm.

'You didn't keep it down?' asked Marthe.

'I told you I couldn't eat.'

'You positively have to see a doctor.'

'I don't want to.'

What could a doctor do? And what would be the point, anyhow? Now that she had been sick she felt fine. It was dark inside her; she gave herself up to the darkness. She thought about a story she had read: a mole felt its way through its underground tunnels; it came out and sensed the clean fresh air; but it could not find out how to open its eyes. She told herself the story another way: the mole in its underground dwelling found out how to open its eyes, and saw that everything was dark. None of it made sense.

Jean-Charles sat at the side of her bed and took her hand. 'Darling, won't you try to tell me what's the matter? I've talked with Dr. Lebel, and he thinks that something has made you very unhappy . . .'

'Everything's fine.'

'He talked about anorexia. He'll be coming presently.'

'No!'

'Well then, snap out of it. Think. You don't get into an anorexic state without a reason: find the reason.'

She pulled her hand away. 'I'm tired. Leave me alone.'

Things to make one unhappy, yes, she said to herself when he had left the room, but nothing serious enough to prevent her from getting up and eating. I had not succeeded in escaping from my prison; I felt it closing round me again as the plane dived into the fog.

Jean-Charles was at the airport. 'Did you have a good trip?'

'Terrific!'

She was not lying; she was not telling the truth. All these words that are said! Words ... At home the children welcomed me with cries of joy, skipping, kisses, innumerable questions. There were flowers in all the vases. I handed out dolls, skirts, scarves, albums and photographs, and I began to tell the story of a terrific journey. Then I put my clothes away in my wardrobe. I did not have the sensation of playing the part of the young wife who returns to her home: it was something worse. I was not a picture; but I was not anything else either: nothing. The stones of the Acropolis were not more foreign to me than this flat. Catherine alone ...

'How is she?'

'Very well, I think,' said Jean-Charles. 'The psychologist would like you to telephone her as soon as you can.'

'All right.'

Catherine and I talked: Brigitte had invited her to spend the Easter holidays with her in a house belonging to her family near the Lac des Settons; did I agree? Yes. She had been sure I should say yes and she was pleased. She got along very well with Mme Frossard: she drew things there, or played games—she had fun.

Maybe the mother-psychiatrist jealousy is common form: at all events I did not escape it. I had seen Mme Frossard twice, without liking her: she was agreeable, she seemed competent, she asked shrewd questions, quickly recording and listing the answers. When I left her the second time she knew almost as much about my daughters as I did. Before leaving for Greece I telephoned her: she told me nothing—the treatment had scarcely begun. 'And now?' I wondered, ringing her bell. I was on the defensive: barbed wire all over. She did not seem to notice it and she explained the position in a cheerful voice. Broadly speaking, Catherine had a good emotional balance; she loved me immensely, and she was very fond of Louise too; she was not fond enough of her father, who would have to be asked to make an effort. There was nothing disproportionate about her feelings for Brigitte. Only Brigitte was older and precocious; she had had conversations with Catherine that had disturbed her.

'Yet she had promised me to take care; and she's a very straight, decent child.'

'But can you really expect a little girl of twelve to weigh her words exactly? Perhaps she does keep certain things to herself; she tells others that worry Catherine. Her anxiety is staringly obvious in her drawings, her association of ideas and her replies to tests.'

To tell the truth I knew it. I had no need of Mme Frossard to be aware that I had asked the impossible of Brigitte: friendship implies speaking without restraint— speaking from the heart. The only way of protecting Catherine from her was preventing the two children from seeing one another: that was the conclusion Mme Frossard had come to. In this case there was no question of one of those irresistible childish passions where sudden interference is dangerous. If their meetings were spaced out tactfully Catherine would not be badly upset. I was to arrange things so that between now and the summer holidays they should see one another less and that next year they should no longer be in the same class. It would also be a good thing if I were to find other friends for my daughter, younger ones.

'You see! I was right,' said Jean-Charles in a triumphant voice. 'It was that child Brigitte who upset Catherine.'

I can still hear that voice; I can still see Brigitte, with

the pin stuck in her hem—'*Bonjour, m'dame.*' And the knot tightens in my throat. It is a precious thing, a friendship. If I had a friend I should talk to her instead of lying here spiritually exhausted.

'In the first place we shall keep her for Easter.'

'She will be heart-broken.'

'Not if we suggest something more attractive.'

Jean-Charles' mind began to work. Catherine was fascinated by the photographs that I had brought back from Greece: well then, we should take her to Rome with Louise. When we came back we should have to find her things to do that would take up her time and her attention—sports, dancing. Riding! That was a terrific idea; even from the emotional point of view. Replace a friend by a horse! I argued. But Jean-Charles had made up his mind. Rome and riding-lessons.

Catherine looked puzzled when I talked to her about the journey to Rome. 'I promised Brigitte; it's going to hurt her.'

'She'll understand. A journey to Rome—that doesn't happen every day. Don't you want to go?'

'I should have loved to go to Brigitte's.'

Her heart was sad. But once she was in Rome she would be absolutely delighted, that was for sure. She would scarcely think about her friend at all. With a little skill she would have forgotten her entirely by next year.

Laurence's throat tightened. Jean-Charles should never have talked about Catherine's case in public the very next day. Betrayal, violation. What romanticism! But she was overcome by a kind of shame, as though she had been Catherine and had overheard what they had said. Her father, Marthe, Hubert, Jean-Charles and she were all having dinner at Dominique's. (Mama acquiring a taste for family parties! The world holds no more wonders now! And Papa's marked civility towards her!)

'My sister told me about an exactly parallel case,' he said. 'In the fourth form one of her best pupils made friends with an older child, one whose mother was a

145

Madagascan. Her whole outlook upon the world was changed; so was her character, too.'

'Were they separated?' I asked.

'As to that, I don't know.'

'If you consult a specialist, it seems to me that you ought to follow his advice,' said Dominique. 'Don't you think so?' she asked Papa with an air of deference, as though she thought his views of the utmost importance.

I could understand that she was touched by his concern for her—she had such an urgent need for friendship and esteem. What made me uncomfortable was the fact that he let himself be taken in by her little ways.

'It would seem reasonable.'

That hesitating tone. Yet at Delphi, when we were watching the dancing child, out of her mind with music, he had agreed with me.

'In my opinion the problem lies elsewhere,' said Marthe. Once again she said that for a child a world without God was impossible—there was no living in it. We had no right to deprive Catherine of the comforts of religion. Hubert ate in silence. No doubt he was working out some tortuous exchange of key-rings, his latest craze.

'But still it is very important to have a friend!' I said.

'You got along very well without,' replied Dominique.

'Not so well as you think.'

'Well, we'll find her another,' said Jean-Charles. 'This one isn't suitable, since Catherine cries, has nightmares, and does badly at school, and since Mme Frossard finds her somewhat disturbed.'

'We must help her regain her balance. But not by separating her from Brigitte. Come, Papa, at Delphi you said it was normal to be upset when you begin to discover the world.'

'There are things that are normal and that it's still better to avoid: it's normal to cry out if you burn yourself. But for all that it's better not to burn yourself. If the psychologist thinks her disturbed...'

'But you don't believe in psychologists!'

I felt my voice getting louder. Jean-Charles looked at me angrily. 'Listen, since Catherine agrees to go away with us without making a fuss about it, don't you go and make one.'

'She makes no fuss?'

'Absolutely none at all.'

'Well, then!'

Both her father and Dominique said it together, this 'Well, then!' Hubert wagged his head with a knowing air. Laurence forced herself to eat but it was then that she had the first spasm. She knew she was beaten. You can't be the only one in the world who is right; she had never been arrogant enough to think so. (There were Galileo, Pasteur and the others Mlle Houchet told us about. But I don't take myself for a Galileo.) So at Easter —she would certainly be well again by then, it was only a matter of a few days; for a few days you loathe the idea of eating and then of course it ends by settling down—they would take Catherine to Rome. Laurence's stomach went rigid. Perhaps she would not be able to eat for a long while. The psychologist would say she was making herself ill on purpose because she did not want to take Catherine away. Ridiculous. If she really did not want to she would refuse: she would fight. They would all be forced to give way.

All. For they were all against her. And now the picture that she rejected more violently than any was bearing down upon her once again—the picture that re-formed the minute her watchfulness slackened, the picture of Jean-Charles, Papa, Dominique, all grinning as though they were part of an American poster in praise of a brand of oatmeal. Reconciled, giving themselves up to the joys of family life. And the differences that had seemed so essential were not really of any importance after all. She alone was different; rejected; no good at living; no good at loving. With both hands she gripped the sheet. What she dreaded worse than death was upon her—one of those moments when everything crumbled. Her body was a stone: she wanted to shriek, but stone has no voice; nor tears.

I did not want to believe Dominique: it was three days after that dinner, a week after our return from Greece. She said to me, 'Just imagine: your father and I are thinking of living together again.'

'What! You and Papa?'

'Does it surprise you all that much? Why should it? After all, we do have a great deal in common. An entire past, to begin with; and you and Marthe and your children.'

'Your tastes are so different.'

'They were. We have altered a little as we've grown older.'

Keep calm, keep calm, I said to myself. There were spring flowers in the drawing-room—hyacinths, primroses. Presents from Papa, or was she changing her style? Who was she copying? The woman she wanted to become? She talked. I let the words flow over me, still withholding belief: she had invented things so often. She needed security, affection, respect. And he felt that for her, very strongly. He realized that he had misjudged her and that her social life and ambition were a kind of vitality. And as it happens he needed someone with a great deal of vitality in his life. He felt lonely; he was bored: books, music, culture—they were all very fine, but they were not enough to fill an existence. It had to be admitted that he was still very attractive. And then he had developed. He understood the sterility of a negative attitude. Seeing that he knew so much about parliamentary life she had suggested that he should take part in a debate on the radio. 'You can't imagine how pleased he was.' The even, contented voice flowed on in the mild warmth of that same drawing-room which had echoed with those horrible cries. 'You bear things, you know; you bear them.' Gilbert had been right. You cry out, you weep, you wring your hands, as though there were something in life worth these cries, these tears, these convulsive motions. And it's just not true. Nothing is irreparable because nothing is of any importance. Why not stay in bed all your life?

'But come,' I said, 'you think Papa's life so dreary!'

I did not understand. Dominique had not suddenly changed her opinion of Papa: she had not become converted to his view of the world nor was she resigned to sharing what she called his mediocrity.

'Oh, I shall keep my own!' she said eagerly. 'We are entirely in agreement upon that point—separate activities and separate friends for each.'

'A kind of peaceful coexistence?'

'If you like to put it that way.'

'Then why not just see one another from time to time?'

'You really know nothing of the world; you don't understand at all!' said Dominique. For a moment she remained silent: it was clear that what she was turning over in her mind had nothing pleasant about it. 'I've already told you that socially a woman without a man is *déclassée*—she's lost her position, she's neither here nor there. I know that people are already saying that I have a gigolo; and what's more there are some young men who have suggested themselves.'

'But why Papa? You might have chosen a more brilliant man,' I said, emphasizing the brilliant.

'Brilliant? Compared with Gilbert nobody is brilliant. It would look as though I were satisfied with a poor imitation. Your father is something completely different.' A thoughtful look passed over her face, one that matched the hyacinths and the primroses. 'A married couple who come together again after a long separation so as to face old age together—people may be surprised, but they won't snigger.'

I was less sure of that than she: but now I understood. Security, respectability: that was her primary need. Any new affair or liaison would bring her down to the level of an easily-bedded woman and it was not as simple as all that to find a husband. I had a glimpse of the character that she was going to build for herself—a woman who had reached the top, a successful woman, but one who had turned away from frivolity, preferring more esoteric, more difficult, more intimate forms of happiness.

But did Papa agree? Laurence went to see her father that very evening. The bachelor's flat that she liked so, with its papers and books lying about in heaps and its old fashioned smell. Almost immediately she asked, with a forced smile, 'Is it true what Dominique says, that you're going to live together again?'

'Well, however surprising you may find it, yes.' He seemed rather embarrassed: he was remembering what he had said about Dominique.

'Yes, it does surprise me. I confess. You were so very much attached to your solitude.'

'I shall not be obliged to give it up if I move in with your mother. Her flat is very big. Naturally at our age we both of us need our independence.'

Slowly she said, 'I suppose it's a good idea.'

'I think so. I live too much turned in upon myself. After all one does have to keep in touch with the world. And Dominique has matured, you know: she understands me far better than she used to.'

They had talked about various things, about other people and about their journey to Greece. That evening she had thrown up her dinner: she had stayed in bed the next day, and the next, overwhelmed by a chaotic sequence of pictures and words that raced through her head, fighting among themselves like Malay krisses in a closed drawer (if you open it, everything is in order). She opened the drawer. I am just plainly jealous. Oedipus not coped with properly, my mother still my rival. Electra, Agamemnon. Was that why Mycenae stirred me so? No. No. Stuff and nonsense. Mycenae was beautiful and it was its beauty that moved me. The drawer was closed again: the krisses fought. I am jealous but above all, above all ... She breathed too fast, she panted. So it wasn't true that he possessed wisdom and joy and that his own inner glow was enough for him! She had blamed herself for never having been able to discover that secret —perhaps after all it had never had any existence at all. It did not exist: she had known that ever since Greece. I've been *deceived*. The word stabbed her. She pressed her handkerchief against her teeth as though to hold back the cry that she was incapable of uttering. I am bitterly disappointed. I have cause to be. 'You can't imagine how pleased he was!' And Papa, 'She understands me better than she used to.' He had felt flattered. *Flattered*, he who used to look down upon the world from such a height of smiling detachment, he who knew the emptiness of all things and who had found serenity on the far side of despair. He, the one who would never compromise, was going to talk on that radio which he accused of lying and of servility. He was not a being of another kind. Mona would say, 'They're all the same, love. Two peas in a pod.'

She dozed off, exhausted. When she opened her eyes again Jean-Charles was there. 'Darling, you really must agree to see a doctor.'

'What for?'

'So that you and he can talk: he'll help you understand what's happening to you.'

She started violently. 'No, never! I shan't let myself be manoeuvred.' She shouted, 'No! No!'

'Gently, now.'

She fell back on her pillow. They would force her to eat; they would make her swallow it all. All what? All that she vomited out, her life, the lives of the others with their phoney loves, their stories about money, their lies. They would cure her of her rejection and her despair. No. Why this no? What did it profit the mole to open its eyes and see that everything was dark? Close them again. And what about Catherine? Sew her eyes up? 'No,' she cried aloud. Not Catherine. I shan't let what has been done to me be done to her. What have they made of me? This woman who loves no one, who is indifferent to the beauties of the world, who cannot even weep—this woman that I vomit forth. Catherine: on the contrary— open her eyes at once and maybe a gleam of light will make its way through as far as her; maybe she will get herself out of it. Out of what? Out of this night. Of ignorance, of uncaring. Catherine ... She sat up suddenly. 'They shan't do what they've done to me to Catherine.'

'Calm down.' Jean-Charles took her wrist; his look was wavering as though he would like to call for help. So authoritative, so certain of being in the right, and the slightest unexpected thing is enough to frighten him.

'I shan't calm down. I won't have anything to do with any doctor. It's all of you who are making me ill and I shall cure myself on my own because I shan't give in to you. Where Catherine's concerned I shall not give in. As for me, it's all over: I've been had. All right, fine, I can take it. But she's not going to be maimed. I won't have her deprived of her friend: I want her to spend her holidays at Brigitte's. And she's not going to see this psychologist any more.'

Laurence threw back her bed-clothes; she got up and slipped on a dressing-gown; she caught Jean-Charles' dismayed look. 'Don't call the doctor: I'm not raving. I'm saying what I think, that's all. Oh, don't put on that sort of a face!'

'I don't understand a thing of what you're saying.'

Laurence took a grip on herself and spoke in a reasonable voice. 'It's easy enough. I'm the one who looks after Catherine. You do come in now and then. But I'm the one who brings her up and it's for me to take the decisions. I am taking them. Bringing up a child doesn't mean turning it into a pretty picture ...' In spite of herself Laurence's voice was rising; she talked on and on, she was not quite sure what she was saying but it did not matter—what did matter was to shout louder than Jean-Charles and all the others and to reduce them to silence. Her heart was beating furiously, her eyes blazed. 'I have taken my decisions, and I shall not yield.'

Jean-Charles seemed more and more taken aback; in a soothing tone he murmured, 'Why didn't you tell me all this before? It wasn't worth making yourself ill. I had no idea you took this business so much to heart.'

'To heart, yes; maybe I have no heart left, but this business—yes, I do take it to heart.'

She looked him straight in the eye. He turned his head away. 'You ought to have spoken to me before.'

'Perhaps. In any case I have now.'

Jean-Charles is stubborn; but fundamentally he doesn't take this friendship between Catherine and Brigitte very seriously—the whole thing is too childish to interest him much. And it was no fun, five years ago; he doesn't want me to crack again. If I stand firm I shall win. 'If you want war, war it shall be.'

He shrugged his shoulders. 'War: between us? Who do you think you're talking to?'

'I don't know. That depends on you.'

'I've never gone against your wishes,' said Jean-Charles. He thought for a while. 'It is quite true that you spend much more time looking after Catherine than I do. In the last resort it's for you to decide, and I've never maintained that it is not.' In an ill-tempered voice he added, 'It would all have been much simpler if you had explained right away.'

She forced a smile. 'I was wrong. I don't like going against your wishes either.' They were silent. 'Well, that's agreed, then?' she said. 'Catherine spends her holidays at Brigitte's?'

'If that's the way you want it.'

'Yes, it is.'

Laurence brushed her hair; she did something towards

putting her face to rights. As far as I'm concerned the game's over, she thought, looking at her reflection—rather white and haggard. But the children will have their chance. What chance? She did not even know.

Simone de Beauvoir

She Came to Stay
The passionately eloquent and ironic novel she wrote as an act of revenge against the woman who so nearly destroyed her life with the philosopher Sartre. 'A writer whose tears for her characters freeze as they drop.' *Sunday Times*

Les Belles Images
Her totally absorbing story of upper-class Parisian life. 'A brilliant sortie into Jet Set France.' *Daily Mirror*. 'As compulsively readable as it is profound, serious and disturbing.
Queen

The Mandarins
'A magnificent satire by the author of *The Second Sex*. *The Mandarins* gives us a brilliant survey of the post-war French intellectual . . . a dazzling panorama.' *New Statesman*. 'A superb document . . . a remarkable novel.' *Sunday Times*

The Woman Destroyed
'Immensely intelligent, basically passionless stories about the decay of passion. Simone de Beauvoir shares, with other women novelists, the ability to write about emotion in terms of direct experience . . . The middle-aged women at the centre of the three stories in *The Woman Destroyed* all suffer agonisingly the pains of growing older and of being betrayed by husbands and children.' *Sunday Times*

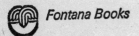 *Fontana Books*

Anthony Powell

'Powell is very like a drug, the more compelling the more you read him.' *Sunday Times*

A Dance to the Music of Time

'The most remarkable feat of sustained fictional creation in our day.' *Guardian*

A Question of Upbringing
A Buyer's Market
The Acceptance World
At Lady Molly's
Casanova's Chinese Restaurant
The Kindly Ones
The Valley of Bones
The Soldier's Art
The Military Philosophers
Books Do Furnish a Room
Temporary Kings
Hearing Secret Harmonies

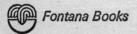 *Fontana Books*

Fontana Russian Novels

A Country Doctor's Notebook Mikhail Bulgakov
'Based on his experiences as a young doctor in the chaotic years of the Revolution. About 1000 miles from the lecture theatre and 30 miles from the nearest railway, he was faced with a bewildering array of medical problems and the abysmal ignorance of the Russian peasant.' *Observer*. 'Wryly funny – and fascinating.' *Sunday Times*

The Master and Margarita Mikhail Bulgakov
'The fantastic scenes are done with terrific verve and the nonsense is sometimes reminiscent of Lewis Carroll . . . on another level, Bulgakov's intentions are mystically serious. You need not catch them all to appreciate his great imaginative power and ingenuity.' *Sunday Times*

The White Guard Mikhail Bulgakov
'A powerful reverie . . . the city is so vivid to the eye that it is the real hero of the book.' *V. S. Pritchett, New Statesman*. 'Set in Kiev in 1918 . . . the tumultuous atmosphere of the Ukranian captial in revolution and civil war is brilliantly evoked.' *Daily Telegraph*. 'A beautiful novel.' *The Listener*

The First Circle Alexander Solzhenitsyn
The unforgettable novel of Stalin's post-war Terror. 'The greatest novel of the 20th Century.' *Spectator*. 'An unqualified masterpiece—this immense epic of the dark side of Soviet life.' *Observer*. 'At once classic and contemporary . . . future generations will read it with wonder and awe.' *New York Times*

Doctor Zhivago Boris Pasternak
The world-famous novel of life in Russia during and after the Revolution. '*Dr. Zhivago* will, I believe, come to stand as one of the great events of man's literary and moral history.' *New Yorker*. 'One of the most profound descriptions of love in the whole range of modern literature.' *Encounter*

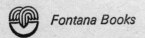 *Fontana Books*

Taylor Caldwell

One of today's best-selling authors, Taylor Caldwell has created a host of unforgettable characters in her novels of love, hate, drama and intrigue, set against rich period backgrounds.

'Taylor Caldwell is a born storyteller.' *Chicago Tribune*

Captains and the Kings

The Romance of Atlantis

The Arm and the Darkness

The Sound of Thunder

Tender Victory

This Side of Innocence

Melissa

The Beautiful is Vanished

Dear and Glorious Physician

Great Lion of God

There Was a Time

The Wide House

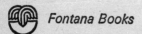 *Fontana Books*

Winston Graham

'One of the best half-dozen novelists in this country.' *Books and Bookmen*. 'Winston Graham excels in making his characters come vividly alive.' *Daily Mirror*. 'A born novelist.' *Sunday Times*

His immensely popular suspense novels include:

Take My Life
The Sleeping Partner
Fortune is a Woman
Marnie
Greek Fire
The Little Walls
Night Without Stars
The Tumbled House
Night Journey

Winston Graham has also written The Poldark Saga, his famous story of eighteenth-century Cornwall:

Ross Poldark
Demelza
Jeremy Poldark
Warleggan
The Black Moon

And historical novels including:

The Grove of Eagles

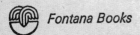 *Fontana Books*

Fontana Books

Fontana is a leading paperback publisher of fiction and non-fiction, with authors ranging from Alistair MacLean, Agatha Christie and Desmond Bagley to Solzhenitsyn and Pasternak, from Gerald Durrell and Joy Adamson to the famous Modern Masters series.

In addition to a wide-ranging collection of internationally popular writers of fiction, Fontana also has an outstanding reputation for history, natural history, military history, psychology, psychiatry, politics, economics, religion and the social sciences.

All Fontana books are available at your bookshop or newsagent; or can be ordered direct. Just fill in the form and list the titles you want.

FONTANA BOOKS, Cash Sales Department, G.P.O. Box 29, Douglas, Isle of Man, British Isles. Please send purchase price, plus 8p per book. Customers outside the U.K. send purchase price, plus 10p per book. Cheque, postal or money order. No currency.

NAME (Block letters)

ADDRESS

While every effort is made to keep prices low, it is sometimes necessary to increase prices on short notice. Fontana Books reserve the right to show new retail prices on covers which may differ from those previously advertised in the text or elsewhere.